# See Me

I0629974

Adrienne Thompson

Pink Cashmere Publishing Company
USA

Edited by Alyndria Mooney

Cover Design by Adrienne Thompson

Printed in the United States of America

First Printing 2012

Copyright © 2012 Adrienne Thompson

ISBN: 0983756988

ISBN-13: 978-0-9837569-8-9

I'd like to extend a special "thank you" to my parents, siblings, and children for being ever supportive of me and my work.

To Alyndria Mooney—the best editor in the world and a pretty good daughter, too, I thank you from the bottom of my heart! I love you.

To my friends and co-workers: thanks so much for your support.

To my Facebook, Twitter, and Goodreads friends: thanks for connecting with me.

I owe a huge debt of gratitude to Orsayor Simmons and Book Referees, Esther Cope, Margie Nesby, Channon Horne, Mia Danielle, Sandra Hall, Cathy Jo, Karla Dozier, Kimberly T. Matthews, Marsha Brown, Stephanie Holston Shelton, Karen McCollum Rogers, Sandra Widener Davis, OOSA Online BookClub, Phoenix C. Brown, La'ChaCha Crawford, Lee Regan O'Neal, Toshana Carter, Akansha Kaira, Danica Nichole Worthy, Ruth Brockman, and many more wonderful people who have been true supporters of my work and have spread the word. If I have omitted anyone's name, please charge it to my head and not my heart. I truly appreciate you all!!

This book is dedicated to those who lose themselves in their love for others. Always remember to love yourself. You're worth it.

## Also By Adrienne Thompson:

*Bluesday*

*Lovely Blues (Bluesday Book II)*

*Been So Long*

*When You've Been Blessed (Feels Like Heaven)*

## Coming soon:

*Little Sister (Cleo's Story)* – A Companion novel to Been So Long

*Been So Long 2 (Body and Soul)*

*My lover is mine, and I am his...*

Song of Solomon 2:16 NLT

Soundtrack provided by Luther Vandross

*"Going In Circles"*

*"See Me"*

*"Hello"*

*"Sugar And Spice"*

*"I Want The Night To Stay"*

*"I'm Gonna Start Today"*

*"Promise Me"*

*"Killing Me Softly"*

*"Like I'm Invisible"*

*"Anyone Who Had A Heart"*

*"Reflections"*

*"So Amazing"*

*"The Night I Fell In Love"*

*"Sometimes It's Only Love"*

*"Too Far Down"*

*"Heaven Knows"*

*"The Best Things In Life Are Free"*

*"A House Is Not A Home"*

*"Love Forgot"*

*"Think About You"*

*"Forever, For Always, For Love"*

*He stood about 5'11" tall. He was thin, but fit. At first glance, I thought he was of mixed race or maybe Greek or Italian. It was hard for me to tell. But it was easy to see how handsome he was. His chocolate brown eyes were piercing. He wore his shoulder-length jet-black, silky hair loose. I remember staring at him and wondering just who this handsome man was.*

*In a time when guys were wearing brightly-colored, oversized Cross Colours and FUBU outfits, he wore tight jeans, t-shirts, and blazers. His customary footwear was high-top Converse sneakers. He was far ahead of nineties fashion.*

*He looked different. He was very different, and that's what I liked about him. From the second I laid eyes on David Moy, I was totally and completely captivated by him. I knew he had to be mine, no matter what it took.*

## *One*

## "Going In Circles"

*I* sat on my front porch and closed my eyes as the warm rays of the sun bathed my face. I smiled. It was a small smile, but it was a smile nonetheless. Freedom. That's what the sun felt like. Freedom. For so many years, I'd coveted it, craved it. Now, I had it and I honestly did not know what to do with it.

I opened my eyes and surveyed the yard. The grass was in terrible need of a trim. David always took care of the yard. David always took care of everything. David—his name alone brought back the sound of the gun going off and the smell of gun powder. *David*.

The buzzing of my cell phone interrupted my thoughts. I checked the caller ID and smiled again. "Hello?"

"Hello, Mother?" It was my son, Jason.

"Of course. Who else would it be?"

"You didn't *sound* like yourself."

"Oh."

"How are you?"

I hesitated. "I'm fine." It was a lie and I was sure that he knew it.

"You don't sound fine."

"Well, I am."

He sighed. "Okay, if you say so. What have you been up to?"

"Nothing really. Reading, sorting through some things, thinking. I'm sitting on the porch right now. The grass is getting so high..."

"Mother, you should move. I told you, you shouldn't be worrying yourself with the upkeep of that house."

"It's my home, Jason. *Our* home."

"My home is in Chicago, now. I wish you'd take me up on my offer. I've plenty of room."

I smiled. That was my boy. Always worried about me. "I'm fine, Jason. Really, I am."

He sighed. I was frustrating him. "Okay, well, I've got to go. I love you, Mother."

"I love you, too. We'll talk later."

I laid my phone down and shook my head. I walked back into the house, into the living room. Reminders of David surrounded me. Pictures, awards, certificates. I sat on the sofa. Freedom—I had the freedom to cry.

So I cried.

## *Two*

## "See Me"

*I* walked up and down the aisles of Dickerson's Bookshop and eyed the titles. Mystery, romance, non-fiction—almost every section held titles by Dr. David Moy. I stopped and leafed through a copy of *Prose and Poise*, David's first book. A full volume of beautiful poetry and short stories dedicated to me. I held it in my hand and closed my eyes. I could see David sitting at that old desk in our tiny studio apartment, his pen moving at a feverish pace.

I quickly opened my eyes and replaced the book on the shelf. I continued browsing, finally selecting a couple of classics, *A Tale of Two Cities* and *The Count of Monte Cristo*, and headed to the counter. I smiled at Kerry, the clerk. Her parents owned the store, and I'd known her since she was a pre-teen. Now, she was in college and she always worked in the store during the summertime.

She greeted me with a bright smile. "Mrs. Moy! So good to see you!"

I smiled at her newly acquired eastern accent, undoubtedly a result of so much time spent away at college. "Good to see you, too, dear."

She took the books and looked up at me. "Classics, huh? None of Dr. Moy's books? But then again, I guess you already own them all. Probably have a library full of original first draft copies. I'm sorry, by the way, for your loss. My parents always said he was a genius. He'll be missed…"

My mind trailed off as she continued to ramble on. I'd heard those words so many times before, "I'm sorry for your loss," or "Dr. Moy was a genius," or "The literary world will never be the same." It had been a year and the accolades and condolences continued to pour in.

"How's Jason?" she asked. I snapped out of my thoughts in time to hear my son's name.

"He's well."

"I had the biggest crush on him. He is so handsome! Is he still in school?"

"Actually, he's finished his Master's Degree and he's teaching now."

"Wow. He was always so smart. Just like Dr. Moy."

*Not like David. No one is like David*, I thought. I handed her the money and turned to leave.

"Goodbye, Mrs. Moy."

I smiled. "Goodbye."

~*~

I walked to the front door with a frown. It was ten on a Friday morning and I was still in bed when I heard the doorbell. I'd been unable to sleep the previous night. Too many thoughts were running through my mind. Thoughts of David and the day he died.

I looked through the peep hole. I didn't recognize the dark, tanned white man on the other side of the door. *Probably one of David's fans.* "Who is it?" I asked through the closed door.

"Mrs. Moy? My name is Brad Coulter. I'd like to speak with you about your late husband."

I was sure he was a reporter. I sighed. "Who'd you say you were with?"

"I didn't, but I'm with *Literary Times* magazine. We want to do a piece on Dr. Moy's life and death."

"Well, I'm sorry. I'm not doing any interviews."

"Mrs. Moy, your husband had so many admirers of his work, and his death was so tragic. They'd love to hear from you. They want to know how his suicide has affected you."

"I am not doing interviews! Please leave!" I shouted. I turned and walked away from the door and his voice became a muffled blur. "Mrs. Moy...Mrs. Moy..."

I slowly climbed the stairs to my bedroom. *I'll have to start locking the gate*, I thought. I laid down in the bed and tightly shut my eyes. I didn't want to talk about David or his life or his death. Why couldn't people understand that? Why couldn't they just leave me alone?

I listened to my cell phone as it vibrated against the nightstand. I knew it was Jason. I had no other family. No friends. Friends would've been a liability to my marriage with David. I pulled the covers over my head and finally found the sleep that had eluded me for so long. When I awakened that evening, Jason was standing over my bed with a concerned look on his face.

## *Three*

## "Hello"

*Startled*, I sat up in the bed and tried to get my bearings. I looked at Jason and rubbed my eyes. "Jason?" I asked, thinking that maybe I was seeing things. Maybe I was losing my mind.

"Mother! Thank God you're alright. I was worried sick! I've been calling and calling. The last time I couldn't get you on the phone..." he hesitated and then added, "I thought something had happened to you!"

"Jason, my goodness! I was only asleep for a few hours. You came all the way to Arkansas for nothing. You really need to stop worrying so much! I am fine. It's Friday night and you should be out having fun."

The concern in Jason's eyes deepened. "Mother, it's Sunday evening," he said softly.

I stared at him. "No, it's Friday. I know it is..." I dropped my eyes to the floor as if the glossy wooden planks could offer some explanation as to what was going on.

Jason squatted in front of me. "What's the last thing you remember?"

I shrugged. "There was a man at the front door that morning. He wanted to do an interview. I told him to leave. *I was so tired.* I haven't been sleeping all that well. So, I climbed into bed and fell asleep. But that was Friday. This can't be Sunday. That would mean that I've been asleep for—"

"*Two days.* Does this happen often?"

I shook my head. "Of course not! There's nothing wrong with me."

"But you've been having trouble sleeping?"

I stared across the room at my reflection in the dresser mirror. "Sometimes..."

Jason shook his head and glanced over at the other side of the bed. *David's* side of the bed. His eyes then travelled to the closet door. "Mother, pack some things. You're coming with me."

I rubbed his cheek. "I'll be fine, really. I can't leave here. I...I need to stay."

He sat down beside me on the bed. I smiled faintly. He was so much like David. He was so handsome. "I know that this house is important to you. But maybe you need a little time away from here, away from the memories. It's been a year and you've hardly left this house. Come to Chicago with me, if not for your sake then for mine. I worry about you, Mother. Please come with me."

I stared at my son for a moment, my beautiful son. He was all I had left in the world. He was everything to me. I reached over and hugged him. "I love you, Jason. I'll do it for you, if it will ease your mind."

He smiled and a relieved look spread across his face. "It will. Thank you, Mother."

~*~

Our flight was smooth and Jason seemed very excited about having me in Chicago with him. I had to admit that I was a little excited myself. I'd been holed up in that house with my memories for a very long time—too long it would seem. Maybe a change of scenery would do me good.

As we pulled up to Jason's apartment building, my eyes widened. It wasn't necessarily dilapidated, but the place left much to be desired. It was an old building which housed four units. Jason said it was only a few blocks from the college where he worked and that he saved a lot of money by walking to work. I wondered if it was even safe for him to be walking in that neighborhood.

Noticing the concern on my face, he gave me a reassuring smile. "It's safe, and besides, I'm just a poor teacher. I don't have anything that anyone would want to steal." The truth was that Jason had inherited half of his father's fortune, so we both knew what he'd said was untrue.

"If you say so, but I think I'll leave the walking to you, my dear son."

Jason chuckled as he pulled my bags from the trunk of his car and led me into the less-than-aesthetic building. "Sorry. The elevator's out of order," he said, giving me a sheepish look. I shook my head as I followed him up the stairs. By the time we made it to his door, I was out of breath. Maybe I *did* need to do some walking.

As he stuck his key in the door, the door to the apartment across the hall opened. I almost dropped my purse at the sight of the young man who emerged from the apartment. He was tall, dark, and *seriously* handsome. Standing there shirtless, looking like a Nubian prince, he took what was left of my breath away.

"Hey, Ben! I want you to meet someone," Jason said. He was smiling at this man as if he were an old friend of the family.

Ben smiled and, although I didn't think it was possible, he grew even more handsome. "Sure. Who've we got here?" he said as he moved closer to us, his eyes trained on me.

"Dr. Bennett Paul, this is my mother, Olivia Moy. Ben's the head of the English department at the college and he owns this building."

I raised my eyebrows as I shook his extended hand. "Oh, well, nice to meet you. Your building has a lot of…uh…character."

Ben laughed heartily. "It's a work-in-progress. Fixing up this old place is my favorite pastime."

I nodded. "I see. Well, it's a pleasure to meet you, Dr. Paul."

"The pleasure is all mine. I can't believe that I'm standing in front of the Olivia Moy. *'Enchantment in bodily form, a beauty so intangible...'*"

I blushed as he recited a portion of *Splendor*, one of David's poems, one of the many he'd dedicated to me.

"You can't be a student of the written verse and not know your late husband's work," he said.

"I see. Well, David would be flattered," I said softly.

"Mother's going to be staying with me for a while," Jason said.

Ben's eyes lit up. "That's great! The two of you will have to join me for dinner one evening."

I smiled. "You cook, Dr. Paul?"

He nodded. "It's *Ben*, and yes, I love to cook. I'm pretty good at it, too. Jason knows."

"Yes, ma'am," Jason said with a nod. "Ben's a great cook."

I raised an eyebrow. "Oh, then I look forward to it."

Ben smiled again. "So do I. Well, I'll let you two get inside so that you can get settled. Great to meet you, Mrs. Moy."

"*Olivia*. Great to meet you, too."

Bennett Paul returned to his apartment and I followed Jason into his. I was pleasantly surprised to find that the interior of the apartment was in stark contrast to the exterior of the building. The pale beige walls appeared to have been freshly painted. From them Jason had hung his high school, college, and graduate school diplomas as well as several pieces of framed African art.

There was a chocolate brown leather sofa and matching chair in the living room accented with oak coffee and end tables. There were three mismatched bookcases in the room all packed full of books, including the only book that Jason had penned. I crossed the room and pulled the copy of Sinner's Stroll from the bookshelf.

I smiled as I rubbed my hand across the book's cover and said, "My favorite book by my favorite author."

He kissed my cheek. "You're my mother. You're supposed to say that."

"I mean it."

"Well, thank you. Let me show you to your room."

I followed him into a small bedroom which had been painted burnt orange. There was an old wrought iron bed and an antique dresser in the room. Sitting in the corner of the small room was a wicker rocking chair. "This is lovely, Jason!"

He smiled. "When I saw this furniture at an estate sale a few months ago, I knew you'd love it."

"I do! You knew I'd come, didn't you?"

"I hoped that you would. Well, take your time and get settled in."

"Okay." I kissed his cheek. "Thank you, son."

"Anything for you."

*Four*

**"Sugar And Spice"**

*I'd* been in Chicago for a week and had spent most of that time asleep. Evidently, I was far more exhausted than I'd realized. I woke up the next Monday morning after Jason left for work, and I showered and dressed and piddled around, tidying up his already neat apartment. I smiled as I dusted the frames of the many photos that lined the fireplace mantle. Jason was very well-traveled, having done missions work in Bolivia and the Sudan. He earned his bachelor's degree from Howard University, his graduate degree from Oxford, and was working towards his PhD at Chicago University. He worked as an English instructor at Chicago Catholic College, a small, private institution. Jason Oliver Moy was my greatest achievement and I was as proud of him as a mother could be of her only child.

I continued to peruse the photos and then I stopped dead in my tracks. I picked up the picture and felt my blood run cold. It was taken at Morehouse College several years earlier. Jason couldn't have been any more than ten-years-old. It was taken the day David received his honorary doctorate degree. I remembered that day well.

*Too well.*

I felt the tears before I even realized I was crying. Memories could sometimes be so cruel. There were so many things I wished my mind would let me forget. So much pain, so much agony that just seemed to loom over my head like a dark cloud, following me wherever I went.

I heard a knock at the door, quickly replaced the picture, and wiped my face. I didn't want Jason to see me crying. I pasted on my best smile as I opened the door. "Did you forget your key?" I asked before I realized that it was Ben—not Jason—who had knocked. "Oh, um…" I added. Bennett Paul stood before me looking like a male model in a navy blue three-piece suit.

He looked startled as well. "Sorry to bother you, Mrs. Moy, but I let Jason borrow one of my literary journals, and I really need it for one of my classes today."

"Oh, well you're welcome to come in, but I have no clue where to look for it."

He smiled. "It's okay. He told me to look on the coffee table."

I backed out of the doorway, allowing him into the room. As he passed me, the scent of Dial soap and Jergen's lotion filled my nostrils. No cologne, but he still smelled heavenly. He leaned over and rifled through the pile of magazines on the table. I watched as his red tie hung freely. Bennett Paul was strikingly handsome with smooth dark brown skin, thick black hair cut close to his scalp, and a smile that could break millions of hearts. He was tall and muscular and that suit fit him perfectly. He was gorgeous and young—too young for me.

He stood up straight and smiled. He held the periodical up and said, "Aha, got it! Thank you, Mrs. Moy—uh—Olivia."

I smiled and hoped that he hadn't noticed me staring at him. "You're welcome."

I walked him to the door, but he hesitated at the threshold. He looked me in the eyes and said, "You know, I've never met an actual muse before. I totally understand why Dr. Moy was so inspired by you. You are absolutely, *breathtakingly*, beautiful."

I was shocked by his statement, so shocked that I was left speechless.

He smiled again. "Thanks again, Olivia. Now I owe you two dinners," he said, holding up two fingers.

I watched him walk down the hall with a gait of pure confidence and then I retreated into the apartment. I closed the door, walked into the bathroom, and inspected myself in the mirror. The same smooth brown skin, the same almond-shaped eyes, the same button nose and pouty mouth stared back at me. I rubbed my hand across my hair. I was beautiful, I knew I was. I'd always known it. But the way Bennett Paul had spoken of me made me feel like I was in a league with Helen of Troy, or at least Halle Berry.

I looked down at my body. Gone was the thin figure of the seventeen-year-old girl who'd caught David Moy's eye so many years ago. Instead of a size six, I wore a size sixteen and the pink sundress I was wearing was accenting all of the wrong spots. I sighed. What was the use? I was the widow of a man who'd loved and adored me up until the day he died. Where would I find something better than that?

~*~

I walked across Chicago Catholic's neat campus and strolled into the stately brick building that housed the English department, making my way down the hallway to Jason's office.

I smiled as I spied the placard outside his door that read, *Jason Moy, M.A. English Instructor*. Pride bubbled to the surface as I knocked on the frosted glass window of the door. I knocked twice more and then decided it wasn't a good idea to show up announced.

*Maybe he's in class.*

I turned to leave, ran right into someone, and dropped the small basket of muffins I'd baked that morning. I quickly squatted and began to clean up the mess. "I'm sorry...I didn't see you," I said without looking up.

I felt a hand on my shoulder. "Let me get it." I recognized the voice. Bennett Paul quickly scooped up the muffins and the basket. We both stood up and I said, "Thank you."

"I take it that these are for Jason? I'm sorry," he said.

I shook my head. "I...it's okay. He's not here."

Ben nodded. "He's in class. He should be here shortly. You can wait for him in my office."

I hesitated. Why, I don't know. But I'd walked three blocks, so I decided to take him up on his offer. I followed him into his large office and took in my surroundings. Most of the room was taken up by a huge cherry wood desk and high-backed executive chair. I settled into one of the burgundy cushioned chairs that sat in front of his desk and eyed the diplomas from Morehouse, UCLA, and Stanford that hung on his wall alongside framed playbills and posters of classic black films. When I turned my attention back to Ben, he was staring at me.

Ben quoted another of David's poems: *I breathe her. She is the morning dew. The brilliance of a summer's sunset pales in comparison to her loveliness.*

I smiled. "You are truly a David Moy fan, aren't you?"

"Always have been. I'm a fan of his muse as well."

I shifted my gaze from Ben's smiling face back to the posters and playbills adorning the walls. "You enjoy black theater?" I asked.

He nodded. "Actually, my bachelor's degree is in African American literature with a minor in African American drama."

"Dr. Paul, if you don't mind my asking, how old are you?"

He laughed. "I'll answer if you stop calling me Dr. Paul."

I blushed. "Sorry. *Ben.*"

"I'm thirty-two. Why?"

"You seem too young to be a dean. You must've been a very focused and determined young man."

"I like to think so."

I smiled and noticed that Ben was looking into my eyes. I looked away.

"I know this is a no-no, but I find it hard to believe that you're old enough to be Jason's mother. How old are you?"

I laughed. "It is definitely a no-no, but since you've already told me your age, I'll tell you mine. I'm forty-two."

"You don't look a day older than twenty-two."

I blushed again. "Thanks."

He checked his watch. "Well, Jason should be in his office by now. I'm really sorry about the muffins. Maybe we could apply the five-second rule."

With a wrinkled brow I said, "Five-second rule?"

"You've never heard of it? If something's on the floor for less than five seconds, then it's still safe to eat."

I laughed. "No. Never heard of it. That's cute."

He plucked one of the muffins from the basket and took a bite. "See, still good."

I raised my eyebrows. "Um, I tell you what. You keep them. My treat."

He nodded, took another bite, and gave me a thumbs-up. "Thanks. They're delicious."

He escorted me back to Jason's office where I found my son seated behind his desk with a wide smile on his face.

## *Five*

### "I Want the Night to Stay"

*I* wrapped the blanket around my legs as I settled onto the sofa. It was a stormy Friday night and although I'd never been afraid of storms, the thunder was so loud and the lightening so frequent that I wished I wasn't in the apartment alone. I glanced at the flashlight I'd placed on the table—just in case.

I was pretty engrossed in a Lifetime movie when the power went out. I sat there in the darkness and closed my eyes. It was quiet except for the rain pelting the roof and the boom of the thunder. Somehow, it seemed peaceful to me. I'd almost dozed off when a knock at the door startled me.

"Mrs.—I mean—Olivia? Are you in there?" A voice called through the door.  It was Bennett Paul.

I picked up the flashlight, draped the blanket over my shoulders, and walked to the door. I opened it and shone the flashlight on him.

"Are you okay in there?" he asked with squinted eyes.

"I'm fine. How are the other tenants?"

"They're all gone. It seems we're the only ones in the building."

I nodded. "Well, I'm fine."

"I'm kind of sorry for sending Jason to that conference and leaving you all alone, especially now."

I smiled. "I'm okay, really. Thanks for checking on me."

"Okay, well, I'll be right across the hall if you need me."

"Alright, thanks." I closed the door and settled back down on the sofa. In the quiet darkness, my mind wandered to thoughts of David and the little apartment we'd lived in when Jason was a baby. I thought about that stormy night, so similar to this night. It was the night that he—

Another knock broke into my thoughts. I picked up the flashlight and answered the door again, knowing instinctively that it was Ben. "Yes?"

"I can't leave you in there alone. I can stay here with you or you can come over to my place. Your call."

I really didn't feel like being alone with my memories, so I said, "Come on in."

~*~

We sat in the dark and chatted for a while. Ben told me about how he grew up in a rough Los Angeles neighborhood. He was the youngest of four kids and the only one to graduate from college. His parents still lived in L.A. and he visited them often. He'd been married once and had divorced after only two years of marriage. He had a six-year-old son who lived in California with his mother.

"I bet you miss your son," I said.

I imagined him nodding in the darkness. "Yes, I do, but it's better for his mother to raise him. It's sad to say, but I…I don't think I was ready for parenthood when he came along."

"What about now?"

"Well, I've matured a lot, but I don't want to uproot him. His mother's a good woman. I was just too young to see that when we were married."

"I see."

"Olivia, can I ask you something?"

"Sure."

"Um…I've wanted to write a book for a long while now…"

"I think you should go for it."

"I'm glad you feel that way. I was thinking of writing Dr. Moy's biography. If you'd be willing to help me, it would be the first and only authorized biography."

I shifted my body on the sofa and rubbed my arms. The room had suddenly grown cold. I opened my mouth to speak but my voice seemed to have disappeared.

"He is so beloved and you...you're an icon. He wrote volumes of beautiful work just for you. Your input would make the project very special."

I found my voice and softly said, "I think you should go now."

"I know that it must be difficult for you to talk about him. I can see that you're still suffering from the loss. I'm sorry if I've upset you."

I stood to my feet and fumbled for the flashlight as I fought back tears. I finally gave up hope of finding it and decided to feel my way to the door. I hadn't made much progress when I ran into the coffee table.

"Damn it!" I yelped as I grabbed my leg.

Ben's flashlight popped on and he hurried to my aid. "Are you okay?"

My voice trembled as I wiped the tears from my cheek and said, "I am fine. Please leave now!"

"Okay. I'm sorry, Olivia. I'll check on you again later."

Ben left and almost as soon as the door shut behind him, the lights popped back on. I turned the TV off and went to bed in tears.

## *Six*

## "I'm Gonna Start Today"

*Persistent* pounding on the front door awakened me from a sound sleep. I drug myself out of bed and begrudgingly wrapped my robe around my pajama-clad body as I walked through the apartment to the living room. "Who is it?" I said grouchily.

"It…it's Ben. Jason called and asked me to check on you. He says you haven't been answering your phone. He's worried."

I snatched the door open. "What day is it?"

"It's Sunday morning."

I shook my head. *"Oh, dear Lord.* Let me call him now." I let Ben into the apartment and went into my bedroom to get my phone. Once I'd assured Jason that I was alright, I sat on the sofa across from Ben. "Thank you, Ben. I'm sorry to be such a bother."

With concern in his eyes he said, "Does this happen often?"

"You mean me sleeping for days at a time? I'm honestly not

sure."

"Did this start after Dr. Moy's death?"

I looked at him for a moment. David's death was not a subject I liked discussing, but I shrugged and said, "I don't know. I haven't slept well since he died, so I'm sure that it must have something to do with it. Maybe I'm just making up for lost sleep."

"I'm sorry about the other night. It was wrong for me to approach you like that."

I nodded. "It's okay."

"Well, since I see that you're okay, I'll leave you. I'll be home if you need anything."

I walked him to the door. "Thank you, again."

I spent most of the remainder of that day alone with my thoughts. Thoughts of David, of my sweet Jason, and of Bennett Paul. Ben was a nice man and he wasn't bad on the eyes, either. I can honestly say that in him, I saw a sense of goodness.

I'd been carrying David's memory, the memories of our life together, alone for so long and I was so very tired. I'd been careful to protect both his memory and his legacy. Maybe it was time to let it all go. Maybe the burden of it all was too much for me to bear.

That evening, I walked across the hall and knocked on Ben's door. When he answered, I said, "I'll make you a deal. If you cook dinner tonight, I'll tell you everything I know about David Moy."

Ben smiled. "Thank you."

~*~

Ben wasn't lying when he said he was a good cook. We enjoyed a delicious meal of T-bones steaks that were so tender, I could cut them with a spoon. Along with the steaks we had loaded baked potatoes and fresh spinach salad, and I enjoyed every morsel.

After dinner, we sat in Ben's minimally decorated, but tidy, living room. He placed a small audio recorder between us and I began to talk.

"I met David Moy in freshman English at the University of Arkansas at Pine Bluff. There were three things I learned about David really quickly: he was very handsome, he was charming, and he was absolutely brilliant. We became fast friends because, honestly, I set my sights on him pretty quickly. Once we got to know each other, he told me that I was the smartest girl he'd ever met. He also told me that I was the most beautiful girl he'd ever seen in his life."

"Well, I can't argue with that. You are very beautiful," Ben said.

I smiled. "Thanks. We'd been together five months when I became pregnant with Jason. Two months later, we were married. David's parents weren't too happy about either event."

"His parents? I've never read much about them."

I nodded. "That's the way he wanted it. The only thing he ever told me was that he was adopted by a white couple. Other than that, he never spoke much about them, but I know they didn't get along too well. I've never even met them."

"Really? You were married to him for more than twenty years."

I nodded. "He didn't want them in our lives. I always thought it was sad, but it explained a lot about David."

"What do you mean?"

"Um…we'll get to that later. Anyway, he said he was never able to locate his birth parents."

"Where are his adopted parents now? I'd like to talk with them as well."

"No idea. He was raised in Memphis. Maybe they're still there. Like I said, I never knew them."

"Okay, so you two got married and then Jason came along and

then you two finished college, right?"

"David finished with a degree in English Lit. It only took him three years. I didn't think that I needed to finish."

"Why?"

"Because I had *David Moy*. I'm ashamed to admit it now, but I kind of worshipped David. He was so handsome, so smart. I felt like he was my dream come true. He was all I'd ever wanted or needed—or so I thought at the time."

Ben nodded. "I see. So, his first job was as a graduate assistant at the U of A—Pine Bluff, right?"

"Yes, but he'd only been working for a couple of months when *Prose and Poise* was published. It quickly gained popularity and he landed a really nice book deal. David had written so many poems and stories that he didn't even have to put forth any effort for the next book."

"*Love, In Words*, the book in which the famous 'Ode to Olivia' can be found."

I nodded and smiled. "Yes."

"'*Warm brown skin, I've found, is my addiction. Lips so full, so anxious for mine. I close my eyes, her breath beckons my surrender. It is she, not me, who matters. I feel her touch from afar, knowing every line and ridge of her fingerprint, committing to memory every inch of her beauty. Her soft murmurs and moans are a symphony to my ears. It is Olivia and Olivia alone that I need. My greatest desire is her nearness. Olivia is my divine pleasure...'"*

I felt a chill. I could almost hear David's voice as Ben recited the poem.

"Do you remember when he wrote that?" Ben asked.

I folded my arms around my own body. "Of course," I said softly.

"Tell me."

I looked past Ben at the clock on the wall. I watched as the seconds ticked away. *Tick...tick...tick...* "Where has the time gone? I...I'm feeling a little worn out. Maybe we can resume tomorrow night?"

Ben nodded and stood from his seat. "Sure. Let me walk you home."

Once inside Jason's apartment, I went straight to bed, but lay there awake for most of the night. My mind was racing as I wondered if I was really ready to tell my story. Was I ready to tell the whole truth and nothing but the truth? And was Bennett Paul ready to hear it?

## *Seven*

## "Promise Me"

*Jason* made it back home late that Monday night and headed straight to work on Tuesday morning. Around noon, I dressed in a pair of jeans and a t-shirt and walked the three blocks to Chicago Catholic College. Once I reached Stallworthe Hall, I headed directly to Dr. Bennett Paul's office. He was in class, and I had to wait nearly an hour for him, but I waited nonetheless.

When he finally arrived, he was surprised to see me. "Olivia! I believe Jason is still in class," he said as he flashed that gorgeous smile of his.

I nodded. "I know. I'm here to see you."

With raised eyebrows, he said, "Oh, okay. Well, come on in." He led me into his office. "What can I do for you?"

"You asked me about 'Ode to Olivia'. I'm ready to tell you now. I'm ready to tell you everything."

"About the poem?"

"About everything…but you mustn't tell Jason. I'll tell him before your book is released."

Ben gave me a confused look. "Okay." He pulled the recorder from his briefcase. "Whenever you're ready."

I took a deep breath, released it, and began. "Jason was three months old when David wrote 'Ode to Olivia'…"

*It was storming that night and I sat on the sofa feeding Jason a bottle as David sat at his desk, writing. He'd been writing for hours, like he'd often do. It was what he loved most and it was very easy for him to get lost in his work. Sometimes I thought he loved writing more than he loved me, though he reassured me that wasn't the case. Sometimes I still had my doubts.*

*When he finally took a break, he walked over to me and sat down beside me. He was smiling brightly. He had a look of accomplishment in his eyes. "I wrote something for you. Would you like to hear it, my love?"*

*I smiled. "Of course." Just to be near him and to hear his voice made me happy, but to hear a work he'd composed for me? That always made me feel very special, very loved. I needed to feel loved.*

*He recited the poem and it was so very beautiful. "I love it," I said as I kissed his cheek. I hugged him and breathed in his scent. I loved him so much.*

*He caressed my cheek. "I'm so glad. It's from my heart. I love you, Olivia. You are everything to me."*

*"I love you, too, David. I'll always love you."*

*He took Jason is his arms and kissed his forehead. "Is he finished feeding?"*

*I nodded. I watched as David took Jason and laid him in his crib. Then he took my hand and led me to the bed. He made love to me in the tender way he always did.*

*We were lying in each other's arms when Jason began to cry. I sat on the side of the bed and wrapped my robe around me. "You can let him cry, you know. It won't hurt him," David said.*

*I smiled as I took Jason into my arms. "I can't stand it when he cries. Besides, he's wet." I changed Jason's diaper and then returned to the bed with David. We were into round two of our lovemaking when Jason's cries interrupted us. I tried to get him, but David wouldn't let me go until he was finished.*

*"I'll get him," he said. I watched him as he took Jason and walked into the small kitchen with him. I assumed he was getting him another bottle. I lay in the bed for a moment and then something told me to get up and check on them. It had to be God, because when I walked into the kitchen, I saw David standing over Jason with a knife in his hand.*

*"What are you doing?" I asked as calmly as I could. Maybe it was nothing. Maybe there was an absolutely rational explanation as to why he was standing over our son with a knife. Surely there was.*

*He looked up at me with the strangest look in his eye, a vacant look. Hard as I tried, I couldn't find David anywhere in those eyes. "He has to go, Olivia," he said softly.*

*I frowned. "What?" Surely I'd heard him wrong.*

*A single tear rolled down his cheek. "He's taking you away from me. He's taking all of your love. I have to get rid of him. He was a mistake. I need to fix things." He placed the point of the knife at my baby's throat.*

*I felt like I was having an out-of-body experience. This could not be happening. Panic hit me like a ton of bricks. I slowly reached for David's arm. "No...no, please, David. Please don't hurt him. He's just a baby. Our baby."*

*He backed out of my reach. "He's taken over everything. You spend all of your time with him. I need you, Olivia, but he has you. It's always about him. Him, him, HIM!" His inexplicable anger was growing at a maddening pace, and he was scaring me to death.*

*I moved closer to him and this time he allowed me to touch him. I placed my hand on his arm. I had to get through to him. "I'm sorry. I...I'll do anything you want me to do. Please...please don't hurt him. Please, David, put the knife down. Please, honey. He's your son. Your blood. You don't want to hurt him."*

*David looked down at Jason as if seeing him for the first time. He'd heard me and I think he fully realized what he was doing. He frowned and then handed Jason to me. He left the kitchen with the knife still in his hand. My knees buckled as I cradled my baby in my arms and leaned against the kitchen counter. I stayed in the kitchen for a few moments, trying to gather my senses, trying to figure out what had just happened and why it had happened. I cried tears of relief and tears of anguish.*

*I was still standing in the kitchen silently thanking God when another feeling of dread came over me—David. I finally walked into our bedroom to find David sitting on the side of the bed with his head hung low. I laid Jason in his crib and sat on the bed next to him.*

*I placed my hand on his shoulder. "I love you both, David, in different ways. He's a baby, he's helpless, and he needs me."*

*David nodded and then held the blade of the knife against the skin of his wrist. "It's me. I don't deserve you or him. I don't even deserve to live." He pressed down on the knife hard enough to draw blood.*

*I clasped my hand to my mouth and with a muffled voice said, "David, please give me the knife. I love you. It would kill me if I lost you. I need you so badly. I'll work harder to make you happy. I promise I will."*

*He looked up at me. His brow was deeply furrowed. Tears were steadily streaming down his face. "You said you'd do anything for me. Did you mean it?"*

*I nodded. "Yes. Anything. Please David, give me the knife, honey. Please..."*

*He dropped the knife and pulled me into his arms. He held me tightly for several minutes. He held me so close to him that I could feel his heart thundering in his chest. When he finally released me, he looked into my eyes and brushed his hand across my hair. "It's only you, Olivia. You're my world. My everything," he said.*

*He kissed me passionately, as if it was our last day on earth and this was the last kiss we'd share. With his kiss he seemed to devour me, all that I was. Suddenly, what had transpired earlier had disappeared from my memory. How kind the mind can be at times. I loved him and in an instant, I forgave him. We were intimate again and again that night and then we both drifted off to sleep.*

*When Jason began to cry later that night, I was afraid to move, afraid of how David would react. The events of that evening came rushing back into my mind like a raging river. My baby needed me and I wanted to go to him, but fear paralyzed me. I just laid there until David finally grew tired of his cries and told me to get him.*

"…and that's what I remember about the night he wrote 'Ode to Olivia'."

Ben had an alarmed look on his face. "He…he tried to kill Jason?"

I nodded.

"Did he ever harm him?"

"No, he promised me he wouldn't touch him as long as I kept my promise and that I did."

"What promise?"

"To do anything for him, anything he wanted." I looked away from Ben and asked, "You won't tell Jason will you?"

He shook his head. "No. You have my word." There was a period of silence, and then Ben said, "I…I don't know how to feel about this. I wasn't expecting anything like this."

"Neither was I, but I knew he was very sensitive. His feelings ran much deeper than most people's."

"Well, I just don't know…"

I stood to leave. "I guess that's enough for now. Maybe we can meet tomorrow."

Ben nodded. "Okay," he said softly.

As I walked back to Jason's apartment, I felt ten pounds lighter. For a great burden had been lifted off of me.

## *Eight*

## "Killing Me Softly"

*While* my revelation may have shocked Ben, it was such a relief for me to get it off of my chest. In more than twenty-four years, I'd never told anyone about that night, about that stain in my memory. Yes, I felt lighter. I'd protected David Moy for years and the weight of that responsibility had been overwhelming.

The next evening, I cooked Jason's favorite dinner—shrimp pasta and garden salad. Over dinner, he filled me in on the literary conference he'd attended and after dessert—vanilla ice cream—he retreated into his bedroom to grade papers. I went across the hall to Ben's apartment for another session. At least that's what it felt like, a counseling session. I sat on his comfortable sofa as he laid the recorder down between us. There was uncertainty in his eyes. I think he may have been regretting his decision to interview me. He admired David and learning these things about him seemed to really have shaken him.

"Are you ready?" he asked.

I nodded. "Are you?"

He shook his head. "I'm not sure…but go ahead."

I sighed. "Okay, let's see. *Love, In Words* was published and sold so many copies that we were able to move to New Orleans and buy a small house. Also around that time, a couple of David's poems were recorded as songs, so he made a good penny in royalties. They were big hits."

"I remember that. They were 'Slowly I Sink' and 'She is Love'. They were beautiful songs. Beautiful songs about you."

I clasped my hands in my lap and stared at them. "Yes, they were. Things were good during that time. We were happy. *David* was happy and as long as he was happy, there was peace."

"Okay, so how did *Her Body's Desire* come about?"

I leaned against the back of the sofa. "That was David's first novel. The publishers wanted another book of poetry and short stories, but David wanted to write a novel. He accepted the advance and when he presented the book to them, they were livid. That is, until they read it. It was so provocative, yet beautifully written, they couldn't turn it down."

Ben nodded. "Yes, I read somewhere that it was the predecessor to the African American erotic fiction movement. Ella, the main character in the book, was she modeled after you?"

"She was modeled after the 'me' that David created. The 'me' that I evolved into."

Ben frowned. "What do you mean?"

I sighed again. "When David told me about his concept for the book, I was very excited. I loved everything he wrote and everything he did. Like I said, I worshipped him and he was my life, my everything…"

*"I want to write a book about a black woman who is completely in charge of everything in her life, most of all, her body. She knows what she wants, and she's not afraid to demand it," David said excitedly.*

*"That sounds wonderful, David. I can't wait to read it. Am I your muse again?" I asked.*

*He smiled. "Of course. You are my inspiration for everything, Olivia. You are the air I breathe, darling." He kissed me and then added, "We'll need to do much research. Are you willing to help?"*

*I was growing more excited by the moment. Research? Sexual research? I certainly had no problem with that. I could never get enough of David. "Of course. Research sounds like it'll be fun."*

*He kissed me again. "Wonderful! Remember, this woman is a total sexual liberal. There's not much she'd object to doing."*

*I smiled. "There's nothing I'd object to doing with you, darling."*

*His expression transformed into a more serious one. "Is that a promise, my Olivia?"*

*I nodded and raised my right hand. "I solemnly swear to be your sexual liberal, Mr. Moy." Those would prove to be words I'd live to regret.*

*About a week later, David had finished his outline for the book and he told me that the main character's name would be Ella LaVeaux. He said he needed me to become Ella, but that I'd need to open my mind and free myself of any and all inhibitions. I agreed, of course. By then, Jason was about three-years-old and David had insisted that he be enrolled in preschool so it was just David and I alone in the house throughout the day. That gave us more than enough time for our research.*

*My first lesson in opening my mind came by surprise. At least for me it was. But, it seemed that David had things well planned out. He went out to do some shopping that day, leaving me home alone. I expected him to come back with some sort of gift for me, because he was always surprising me, especially after we were financially stable. Well, he had gone on a shopping spree of a different sort. When he returned, he had a prostitute with him. She was young and blond, barely eighteen years-old.*

*"Darling, this is Lila. I'm going to have sex with her and you're*

*going to watch." He said this as if it was a natural occurrence. As if it was the most normal thing in the world.*

*I was shocked to say the least. "W...What?"*

*He smiled. "You heard me, darling. This is a part of the research we talked about."*

*I shook my head. "B...but David, that's cheating! I can't watch you have sex with another woman! How could you ask me to do something like that?!"*

*His eyes narrowed. I knew I'd made him angry, but what he was asking me to do was ridiculous. "Do you remember your promise, Olivia?"*

*"Yes, but I didn't know that this is what you meant. I...I can't do this."*

*He closed his eyes and shook his head. He moved close to me and pressed his mouth to my ear. In a soft whisper he said, "Olivia...my Olivia. I'm talking about that little deal we made when Jason was an infant. Do you remember? You said you'd do anything I wanted. I've kept my end of the bargain. I've not laid a finger on him." He turned his head and kissed me cheek. "You do remember, don't you?"*

*Tears flooded my eyes. "Please, David. I love you. Don't do this. Don't make me do this."*

*He wiped my tears with his hand. "Come now, you'll love it, darling. It will make things so much better between us."*

*He smiled and then took my hand and Lila's hand and led us both to the bedroom. I sat in a chair and...and—*

"You watched them?" Ben asked, sounding alarmed.

I nodded and wiped a tear from my cheek. Ben handed me a tissue. "I know that to a lot of people it wouldn't have been a big deal, but it destroyed me. Lila was just the first of many. I would to sit there and watch day after day as he slept with different women. Sometimes two at a time. Sometimes he forced me to join them. I'd cry the whole time. Sometimes I wailed. I felt like someone or something had died. I felt like *I* was dying." I stared at the tissue in my hands. "Do you know what David would do when I cried out?"

Ben shook his head.

"He'd cover my mouth. He never...he never stopped. He just covered my mouth and he told those women it was all an act. He told them that I wanted to do it, but I acted like I didn't because it turned him on. He told them he got off on hearing me scream. And the worst part is that I think he really did enjoy seeing me in distress," I said.

Ben shook his head in disgust. "H...how long did this go on?"

I shrugged. "I don't know, three or four months maybe? It went on until he believed that I'd completely opened my mind and shed all of my inhibitions. In reality, I'd grown so numb to the situation that I'd stopped crying." I closed my eyes and shook my head.

Ben moved to the sofa and sat next to me. "I'm so sorry, Olivia."

I looked up at him and saw the sympathetic expression he wore. "It was years ago. I should be over it by now, but back then, I lost a piece of me. That part of my heart that believed in true love and fidelity was totally destroyed." I cried more tears than I knew I had left to cry. Ben sat with me and let me cry for as long as I needed to. He was quiet and he didn't lay a hand on me, but just his presence was comforting. When I'd finished crying, he gave me time to pull myself together and then he walked me back across the hall.

## *Nine*

## "Like I'm Invisible"

"*I* walked in the door with a smile on my face. I'd just dropped Jason off at preschool. I was glad to get back home to have some alone time with David. He'd finally stopped bringing those women home, much to my relief, so the time with him was peaceful. The book was coming along really well and David had been on fire in the bedroom. I didn't think that things could get any better.

"I walked into David's study and saw that he had a visitor, so I quickly began to back out of the room, figuring I'd interrupted a meeting of some sort…"

*"Oh, I'm sorry. I didn't realize you had company. I'll be in the kitchen," I said.*

*"No, darling. Stay. Come on in," David said cheerily.*

*I smiled at the handsome young man who stood next to David and then walked over and kissed David on the cheek. David smiled at me and caressed my cheek.*

*"Jonathon, this is my wife. Isn't she beautiful?"*

*"Yes, she is. Good to meet you, ma'am," Jonathon said as he extended his hand towards me. Jonathon was short with pale skin and curly black hair. He reminded me of a young Tom Cruise.*

*As I shook his hand, David said, "Darling, this is Jonathon. He's a student at Tulane. He's going to help me with my research."*

*I nodded. "Well, it's good to meet you, too, Jonathon."*

*David put his arm around my waist. "Jonathon has agreed to have sex with you today."*

*I felt like I'd been sucker-punched. "W...what?" was all I managed to say.*

*"You and Jonathon are going to have sex, darling," he repeated. He hugged me tightly to him and added, "He says he can go three rounds in a row. We'll see!" David was so excited, almost as excited as I was livid.*

*Jonathon was smiling proudly as I shook my head and whispered, "Um, David? Can I talk to you for a moment?"*

*David's eyes changed in an instant. I'd angered him. I was sure of that. He grabbed my arm tightly, so tightly that he'd leave a bruised handprint behind. He ushered me out of his study and closed the door behind us.*

*"What is it, darling?" he hissed.*

*"I don't want to have sex with that man. I don't want anyone but you. Please...please don't make me do this!" I said, my voice wavering.*

*David sighed as he traced the lines of my neck with his fingertip. "Well, my love, we all must make sacrifices for the creation of art. I sacrificed my happiness for you, now you must do the same. I let you have Jason, now I must have my art. Don't forget about our agreement." His voice was soft and gentle. If not for the acid in his words, I might have been soothed by his voice.*

*I looked him in the eye. My eyes pleaded with his. "David, don't you still love me? Why would you want me to be with someone else?"*

*He gave me a shocked look. "Love? Do I love you? You...you don't know that I love you? Everything I've done was for you." He slapped me and it felt like all of the wind left my lungs at once. I backed away from him, but as I did, he moved closer to me. He tightly grasped my upper arms and said, "Look what you made me do! Darling, it's not real. It's just research. Now, be a good girl and do as I say before I hurt you again." He kissed my sore cheek. "I don't want to hurt you again."*

*I nodded and wiped the tears that began to fall from my eyes.*

*"Good. That's my darling. Go undress. Jonathon and I will meet you in the bedroom."*

*I nodded again and slowly walked down the hall to the bedroom. It felt like I was walking towards a certain doom, but I willed myself to stop crying. I knew that if I continued to cry, things would only be that much worse for me. I undressed and lay across the bed. I felt less than a woman, less than human. When David and Jonathon finally came into the room, I closed my eyes tightly and braced myself for what was to come.*

*"She's gorgeous," Jonathon said.*

*"Yes, she is," David agreed.*

*I heard them chatting as Jonathon undressed, simple small talk. It was almost as if Jonathon was preparing to paint our walls or clean the carpet—nothing special. I kept my eyes closed and pretended that I was somewhere else. I squeezed them tighter when I felt Jonathon climb into the bed with me. My body went as rigid as a board when Jonathon touched me. I willed myself to vacate my own mind. I disappeared. I don't remember a single second of being with Jonathon. The kindness of my mind had returned. All I remember is Jonathon climbing out of bed and the relief I felt knowing that it was over. When I opened my eyes, I saw David giving him some money.*

*Payment for services rendered.*

*"Thank you, Jonathon. Not bad at all. Maybe next time we can get to the other two rounds. Let me show you out," he said. He walked Jonathon to the door and I pulled the covers over my head and just laid there. I still didn't cry. I was afraid to. Afraid I'd make David mad if I did. Afraid that his anger would extend past me to Jason.*

*David came back into the room, humming happily. He pulled the covers off of me and kissed me deeply. "I love you so much. You were wonderful. Watching you with him really turned me on. I have to have you now."*

*I felt so dirty, so filthy. I told him I needed a bath, but he said he wanted me just as I was. He wanted me with another man's scent on my body. We were intimate and he called me his 'Ella' the entire time. To him, I'd finally become Ella and he was happy about it. I don't recall ever seeing him happier than he was that day.*

Ben sat in stunned silence after I'd finished recounting the experience. I gazed out of his living room window at the cars as they sped by on the street below. I shook my head and laughed bitterly.

"Is something funny?" Ben asked quietly.

"No, not really. I was just thinking how foolish I was back then. I let my love for David…I don't know…I just don't know…"

"Olivia, were there other men?"

I scoffed. That was an understatement. "Yes, *several.*"

"Did David ever join in?"

I shook my head. "He'd kiss me or caress me and tell me how much he loved me while those other men were with me, but he never joined in. He never touched them. He wasn't bisexual or gay. It just turned him on to see me with them."

"Um, Olivia? Why didn't you leave David? You sound as if you were miserable."

"I was miserable, but I loved him. As crazy as this may sound, in my mind, it was better to be with him than without him, no matter how bad things were."

Ben leaned over and shut the recorder off. He sighed woefully. "I think we should stop for now. I'm sure you need a break."

"I'm sure you need one, too."

Ben nodded. "As a matter of fact, I do."

## *Ten*

### "Anyone Who Had A Heart"

*I* sat across from Jason at the breakfast table and smiled as he dove into a stack of pancakes. Jason had always been the one thing I'd done right, the one thing I didn't regret. He made all that I went through with David worthwhile. I treasured this time with him and I hated that he would soon know the truth about his father. Jason idolized and adored David.

"Mother, are you alright?" Jason asked.

I snapped out of my thoughts and nodded. "Yes, I'm fine."

Jason took another bite of food and said, "Good. I wanted you to know that I have a date tonight, so you'll have to have dinner without me."

I raised my eyebrows and leaned back in my chair. "A date? Well, Jason, that's wonderful! Who's the lucky lady?"

He smiled. "Her name is Sandra. I met her at Chicago U. She's a very sweet person."

I reached across the table and grasped Jason's hand. "I am so happy for you, son. You go out and have enough fun for both of us, okay?"

Jason squeezed my hand. "Will do."

~*~

I was sitting in Jason's living room with a bowl of buttery popcorn in my lap with plans to spend the evening with *Carmen Jones* and *Imitation of Life* when I heard a knock at the door. I was sure that it was Ben and I was positive that Jason had asked him to check on me.

I opened the door with a smile. "I'm fine."

He gave me a sheepish look. "I'm sorry, but I promised to check on you."

"I figured as much. Jason worries much too much."

"He loves you. Now that I know the sacrifices that you made for him, I think he should worry about you."

I dropped my eyes and shrugged. "Well, come on in. I was about to enjoy all the drama of Preminger's *Carmen Jones*."

Ben followed me into the apartment. "Hmm, a true classic."

I reclaimed my seat on the sofa and nodded. "It sure is. You can watch with me or we could work on the book some more if you want."

Ben sat across from me and rested his left leg across his right knee. "Well, I was wondering…how long have you been in Chicago?"

I shrugged again. "Um, about a month."

"And all you've seen of this city is my building and Chicago Catholic?"

I shook my head. "That's not entirely true. I've seen a lot on my walks to and from the school."

Ben shook his head and sucked his teeth. "Tsk…tsk…shame on Jason Moy."

"Jason's been busy teaching and working on his PhD. You know that…you're his boss. Besides, he's been the perfect host."

"Okay. I've a proposition for you."

"Okay…"

"I'd like to take you out tonight. It's my way of thanking you for sharing your story with me."

I smiled. "What could you possibly have in mind that would make me abandon Dorothy Dandridge and Harry Belafonté?"

He laughed. "Good jazz, fine wine, and dancing."

I gave him a puzzled look. "What?"

"I know a little place across town with the best live band in the land. I'd love to take you there, Olivia."

I suddenly felt uncomfortable. "Um, I…I don't go out, Ben. I'm…I'm a homebody."

"Why?"

I shifted in my seat. "What?" I said absently.

"Why would someone so beautiful want to stay at home all of the time?"

I stared at the floor. "Because…that's the way it's always been. David didn't like to socialize all that much. And when we did go out, it wasn't very enjoyable for me. I'm not comfortable around a lot of people."

"I mean absolutely no disrespect, but David is gone and you're still here. Maybe it's time for you to come out of your shell. You don't have to talk to anyone but me, and I promise to be better company than David."

I looked at Ben for a moment. He was right and I knew it. I was free from David's rule over me, but I wasn't behaving like a free woman. Still, I was afraid. "I…I don't have anything to wear."

"The place has a laid back vibe. Jeans and a blouse will do fine."

I was still uncertain—no, I was *petrified.* To be perfectly honest, I didn't know who I was apart from David Moy. Who exactly was Olivia Moy? Who was she? Would she enjoy a night of music and dancing? I had no idea. I felt like crying. I shook my head. "I just don't know, Ben."

"You'd really be doing me a favor. I haven't been out for a night of fun in weeks." I doubted the validity of his statement. Bennett Paul was so handsome that getting a date could not have been a problem for him.

I closed my eyes and sighed. A million possibilities ran through my head—the same ones that always ran through my head when I was faced with being seen in public. What if someone who knows about my past sees me? One of those men or women? One of my unwanted partners?

"Please, Olivia," he said almost as a whine.

I looked up at him. I didn't want to do it. I really didn't. "Okay," I finally said for some reason. I have no idea why I agreed.

He smiled widely. "Great. I'll be back in an hour."

~*~

I was nervous as I walked into Myra Shae's on Ben's arm. Thankfully we were led to a table located in a dark corner near the rear of the club. The more anonymity the better, as far as I was concerned. We settled down at the table and a few minutes later, were sipping White Zinfandel. We listened to the band and chatted, mostly about the music. Ben was clearly a jazz lover and he really seemed to be enjoying himself. I was having a good time, too, despite myself. At least that was until…

"Olivia, will you dance with me?"

I nearly choked on the wine. Dance? In front of everyone? No way! "Oh no, I don't dance, Ben. Maybe you could ask one of the other ladies in here. I'm sure they'd be more than willing."

He smiled. "But I want to dance with you, not them."

I looked down at the table. "But, I…"

"*Please.* 'Round Midnight' is one of my favorite songs." He gave me an irresistible puppy dog look and I gave in. What else was I supposed to do? We headed to the dance floor and my knees were so shaky. Ben pulled me close to him and it felt strange being held that way by anyone other than David, but it also felt good. Ben was so tall and strong and he held me tightly. I felt completely safe with him and completely comfortable in the warmth of his arms.

Before I knew it, we'd danced through two more songs. I guess I was lost in the music and in Ben's arms. Afterwards, we headed back to our table and enjoyed more wine and conversation. I had a really nice time with Ben. I was glad I'd taken him up on his offer.

Back at his building, Ben walked me to my door. He hugged me and said, "Thank you for a wonderful evening, Olivia."

I kissed him on the cheek. "I had a great time. Thank you."

Ben took my hand and softly kissed it. I smiled again and reached up and rubbed his smooth cheek. He was such a handsome man. He leaned in and brushed his lips against mine so softly, it felt more like a tickle than a kiss. I stared at him—speechless. He wrapped his arms around me and pulled me closer to him. He kissed me deeply. At first I kissed him back, lost for a moment in my undeniable attraction to him. Then everything clicked in my mind, and I fully realized what was happening. I pushed him away and he stumbled backward with a startled look on his face.

"How dare you!" I said in a harsh whisper.

"W…what is it?" He looked even more startled.

"I know what you're doing!"

He moved towards me and I backed away. "Olivia, I like you. I'm attracted to you. What are you talking about?"

"You think that because of the things I told you about me you can have me. Well, I am not a whore!"

He reached for me. "Olivia, I'd never—"

I stumbled backward. "Leave me alone! You'll have to look elsewhere for a good time. I'm not open for business!" I turned and fumbled with my key until I finally ended up dropping it. I squatted to pick it up and collapsed in tears. I sat on the floor, leaned my back against the door, closed my eyes, and covered my face with my hands. I felt Ben sit down beside me.

"I'm sorry, Olivia. I honestly meant no disrespect. I really like you," he said softly. I didn't answer. I just continued to cry. We sat there for a good while before my tears finally ceased.

A few minutes later, I looked up at Ben and gave him a weak smile. "I'm sorry," I said, feeling embarrassed.

He stood and helped me to my feet. "No need to apologize. You've been through a lot. Of course you have issues with trust." He paused and gently, cautiously, placed his hands on my arms. "But I have no intentions of hurting you. I like you...a lot. I really do. And I'm very attracted to you."

I shook my head. "No, you like the icon David created—the

Olivia you read about in his work."

He leaned closer to me. "*No*, I like the Olivia that's standing in front of me right now."

I fixed my eyes on the floor. "Ben, I'm ten years older than you."

"I don't care."

"But you know about my past. What…what if we're out together and one of those men recognizes me? What if one of them approaches us?"

He shrugged. "Then I'll kick his ass."

"Ben…"

He shook his head. "I mean it."

I sighed and stared at him for a moment and then said, "I'd better get inside. Thanks again."

He kissed my cheek. "Goodnight, Olivia."

"Goodnight."

I walked inside to find Jason fast asleep in his bed. I changed into my nightgown and climbed into bed with my mind full of thoughts. Thoughts of Bennett Paul. I quickly blocked those thoughts out. It will never work. I soon fell into a dreamless sleep.

## *Eleven*

## "Reflections"

*When* Ben called and asked me to come to his office at Chicago Catholic, I found myself experiencing a mixture of emotions. I was excited because I liked him and was very attracted to him. I was also afraid, because I was sure he shared those feelings with me. What would become of our relationship? Did we even have a relationship at all? If so, was I ready for a relationship—any relationship? Was I even over David? As I entered the building and headed toward Ben's office, I ran right into Jason.

He kissed my cheek. "Mother! I was just heading out to class. You should've called." I smiled at him but at the same time, I was a little taken aback. Jason possessed so many of his father's mannerisms. The way he'd leaned over and kissed my cheek reminded me of David. It didn't help that he was almost a carbon copy of him, too.

"Oh…well, I'm actually here to see Dr. Paul."

He nodded. "You two are still working on the book?"

"Yes, we are," I said. I'd told Jason that we were working on his father's biography, but had not shared any details.

He hugged me. "Well, I know you'll honor Father's legacy. I'll see you later." I nodded and watched as he walked away with a stride that matched his late father's.

I arrived at Ben's office to find his door open. He was sitting at his desk with his head buried in a book. I knocked lightly on the door facing. Ben looked up and gave me a bright smile. He stood, walked over to me, and kissed my cheek. I sat down as he closed the door.

"How are you, Olivia?"

I smiled. "I'm fine."

"I'm glad to hear it. Thanks for coming."

"No problem. Are we working on the book today?"

"Yes, but I wanna hear about you, today. Tell me about who you were before David Moy."

I sat and thought for a moment. I'd spent most of my life in David's world. Actually, he had been my life. It took a moment for me to remember who I was before him. "Um, I was born in a small town in Louisiana, near New Orleans. My mother was very young when I was born—a teenager. She left when I was three and my grandmother, Bevvie, raised me. Bevvie died right after I started college. I never knew my father. I have no other relatives except Jason.

"I was always considered pretty smart and I graduated at the top of my small high school class. I was awarded a couple of scholarships, including a full ride to the U of A – Pine Bluff."

"Did your mother ever come back? Did you ever see or hear from her again?" Ben asked.

I clasped my hands in my lap. "She came back in a coffin. She was murdered by a jealous boyfriend when I was ten. She was living in Texas at the time."

"Wow, I'm sorry."

I shook my head. "Don't be. I never really knew her."

Ben nodded. "What was your major in college?"

"Chemistry-Pre Med."

"Really?" He said with wide eyes as he leaned back in his chair.

"Yes. When I dropped out of school, I'd earned a 4.0 GPA."

"You had such a bright future."

I looked down at the floor. "Yeah, I did. I'm glad my

grandmother wasn't around to see me drop out. She would've been so disappointed in me."

"Olivia, do you think the fact that you had no family made you cling so tightly to David?"

I nodded. "I'm sure of it. He was literally my world."

"Please don't take this the wrong way, but have you ever sought counseling?"

I frowned. "No. I never thought about it. Do you think I should?"

"I don't know. That would have to be your decision, but I don't think it would hurt. I know of some good Christian Counselors I can put you in touch with, and I really think they could help you."

I shrugged. "Maybe you're right. I'll think about it."

He hesitated and then said, "Tell me about when you first met David."

I gave him a slight smile. I didn't mind talking about our beginning. Those were very happy times. "I'm glad you asked about that, Ben. I'd hate for you to think that our entire relationship was bad, because it wasn't. There was a reason I adored him so. We were very happy for a while."

Ben leaned forward and placed his hands on his desk. "Tell me."

My smile widened. "When David walked into Mrs. Dennyson's freshman English class, my heart stopped. He was so handsome, so gorgeous. He was not like any man or boy I'd ever seen before. He just had this way about him. David was the definition of the word individual. He definitely had his own style, and he was very confident. That was one of the things that drew me to him. That and the fact that he was absolutely brilliant.

"He was obsessed with the written word. Our dates usually consisted of us sitting in the library reading and studying together. We discussed literature a lot, and David told me about all of the books he'd read, hundreds of them! He would amaze me with the way he could recite entire Shakespeare sonnets from memory. He loved Shakespeare. He was partially drawn to me because of how my name related to Shakespeare. He knew the Bible, too. He'd memorized most of the New Testament. He said that the Bible was the greatest piece of literature ever written."

"David was a Christian?" Ben asked with raised eyebrows.

I pondered his question for a moment and then said, "David believed in God. He reverenced Him. I never heard him take His name in vain. But there were also times when, in his own mind, David was the god of his world. I'm sure my total devotion to him fueled that belief."

"What about you, Olivia? Are you a Christian?"

I shrugged. "I was raised a Christian, but to be completely honest with you, my faith has been weak for a long time. There were times in my life when I really felt like God had forgotten about me…deserted me."

"The times when David abused you?"

"Yes, and when my grandmother died and the fact that my mother abandoned me didn't help. And then she was killed. Why would He let so many bad things happen to one person?"

"Because He knows you are strong enough to handle it."

I shook my head. "I'm not so sure about that."

"*You are*, Olivia. You're the strongest woman I've ever met."

"Well, thanks for saying that."

"If you weren't strong, you wouldn't be sitting here today."

I closed my eyes. "Sitting here today came at a price much more costly than you could ever imagine, Ben. But never mind that. What else do you want to know?"

"How was David as a father? You know, as Jason grew up."

"Um, with Jason, sometimes David was there, and sometimes he wasn't."

"What do you mean?"

"There were times when he paid absolutely no attention to Jason. That was usually when he was engrossed in a writing project. Other times, I felt like he almost paid *too much* attention to him. He'd critique everything he did or said. He insisted that Jason speak perfect English at all times—no slang. He'd even scold him for using contractions. It was David who insisted that Jason refer to us as Mother and Father. But by and large, David spent most of Jason's childhood locked up in his study writing or watching his home movies."

"Home movies?"

I sighed. "Oh, I guess I neglected to tell you that he videotaped all of our 'sexual research'. He'd sit in there and watch those tapes of me with those men over and over again and afterwards, he always wanted to be intimate with me—no matter the time of day or night."

Ben's brow furrowed deeply. "He...he taped it?"

I nodded. "It was his documented research." Ben was quiet, so I continued on. "Other times, he was a wonderful father to Jason. He'd read to him, play games with him. David was many different men within one."

"Jason told me that he went to boarding school for a while."

"Yes, David sent him off when he was twelve. I didn't want him to, but he insisted. Then, it was just me and David. Those were hard years for me."

"Why don't we stop here and pick it back up at dinner tonight? We can talk about *Her Body's Fire*, the second installment of Ella's story."

I smiled. "Okay, it's a date."

~*~

We'd just enjoyed veggie quesadillas with sour cream, salsa, and guacamole, and were sitting in Ben's living room with our glasses of wine. Ben held the recorder in his hand and sighed. "Olivia, can I just say something before we begin?"

I took a sip of wine and nodded.

"I am truly sorry for the things you endured with David. If at any time you decide that you don't want me to publish the book, or if you no longer want to discuss your life, I will respect your wishes."

I shook my head. "No. The world sees David as this beloved author who revered women, *especially me*. Everyone should know the entire story, the truth."

"Including Jason? I happen to know that he idolizes his father.

He's pursuing that PhD just to please his father, even though the man's gone."

"*Especially* Jason. I protected him from David's ugly side. I'll always believe that it was the right thing to do, but he's an adult now. He deserves to know the whole truth. If he wants to emulate David, he needs to know that his genius and his success came at a price."

Ben nodded. "Okay, tell me about *Her Body's Fire.*"

"'The second installment of Ella LaVeaux's journey towards total sexual fulfillment.' That was actually the blurb on the back of the book."

"Yes, I've read it."

I raised an eyebrow and tilted my head to the side. "You've read all of his work, haven't you?"

He shrugged and his eyes darted from my face to the floor.

I reached across the coffee table and rested my hand over his. "It's alright. David was a very gifted writer. Everything he wrote came from a passion deep inside of him. You can see pieces of him on every page."

"But it also contains pieces of you."

"Yes," I said softly. I'd never thought of it that way, but it was true. There was as much of me in those books as there was David.

Ben cleared his throat. "Olivia, I've been a fan of David Moy's work for years. But I can't deny that your revelations have changed my view of him and his work."

I dropped my eyes. "I'm sorry. I'm not trying to taint his memory or his work. A part of me still loves him very much and always will. He'll always be the great love of my life. I...I don't want to do anything to disrespect him."

Ben shook his head. "No, don't be sorry. What you're speaking is the truth, and it needs to be told. It just really puts a different spin on things for me."

I nodded and took another sip of wine.

"Ok, you were telling me about *Her Body's Fire*. Was there any 'research' for that book?"

"Yes, by then we'd moved to Memphis—"

"You guys moved a lot didn't you?"

"David liked living in different cities. He found part of his inspiration in the different locales. He said he'd grown bored with New Orleans and Memphis was his hometown. He said he missed it."

"Oh, I see."

I sat my wine glass on the coffee table and continued. "We were living in this beautiful old house in the Evergreen historic district. I think that house was my favorite of those we lived in. It was huge and spacious with hardwood floors and this beautiful backyard. Memphis was nice. It was a city rich in history and southern charm.

"Jason was about six when we moved to Memphis, and David enrolled him in a private school there. Her Body's Desire was a best-seller, and David had just sold the rights to the movie, so we were doing really well financially. Research for the new book started out with him viewing the video tapes of me with those other men and some of me and David being intimate, but he grew bored with them and soon began bringing men home again."

I paused and shook my head. "Every time I had to sleep with those men, I lost another little piece of me. I was so miserable, and then…"

*I knocked on the door to his study and closed my eyes. I held my breath until he opened it. He wore an irritated look on his face as he said, "Yes?" I wasn't supposed to bother him when he was working, but I needed to tell him before Jason made it home from school.*

*"I need to talk to you," I said timidly.*

*He sighed. "I'm working, darling. Can't this wait?"*

*"No…no, I really need to talk to you."*

*He shrugged. "Then talk, Olivia."*

*I eyed him nervously. "Well, can I come in and sit down?"*

*"No. Talk, darling. I'm busy," he said, raising his voice.*

*"I...I'm..."*

*He rolled his eyes. "Damn it! Spit it out, Olivia!"*

*"I'm pregnant."*

*"What did you say?" he asked softly and calmly. Too calmly.*

*I backed away from him. "I'm...I'm pregnant," I repeated.*

*"How could you be so damned stupid, Olivia? Whose is it?" His voice was still calm and soft, barely above a whisper.*

*I shook my head. "How can I know that?"*

*He slapped me so hard that I felt my teeth rattle in my head. I lost my balance and fell to the floor. "You have got to be the dumbest woman on this planet! I thought you were on birth control, dear," he said as he stood over me.*

*I held the side of my stinging face and stumbled to my feet, still off-balance. "I am. I...I don't know how this could've happened."*

*"It happened because you are brainless and careless." This time he balled up his fist and punched me in the jaw. I grunted as his*

knuckles met my face. I don't remember ever feeling such pain before. "You've ruined everything!" He shoved me backwards and I tumbled to the floor again. He kneeled beside me and grabbed my face with his hand. I winced as he gripped my already sore jaw. "We were happy weren't we, Olivia? Weren't we happy?" he asked softly, his face almost touching mine.

I nodded as the tears began to fall. "I'm still happy. I'm happy with you, David."

"Then why would you do something like this? Why, darling? Why do you make me hurt you?" His eyes shone with tears. "I love you, and you insist on making me hurt you." He pulled me into a tight hug.

Maybe it really was my fault. Surely I could've done something to prevent the pregnancy. Maybe I'd been careless. I rested against him. "I'm sorry, David. I didn't mean for it to happen."

He stroked my hair. "Yes, yes, dear. I know. Well, you can't have it. We have to get rid of it. I won't have another child in this house. We already have one too many." He gently cupped my face in his hands and kissed me.

I looked at him, afraid to speak and afraid not to. "M...m...maybe we could put it up for adoption." I didn't want to keep the baby either, but I didn't want an abortion.

David stood to his feet. His expression had totally transformed and his pale skin reddened as he exploded in anger. "Adoption?! Don't be stupid. I was adopted, Olivia, and my life was a living hell! No, let's just put the little thing out of its misery." He kicked me in my side and I screamed. I tried to curl myself up into a ball, but I was too late. The next thing I felt was the toe of his shiny loafer as it met the center of my gut. He kicked me over and over again and I felt the intensity and the force of each and every blow as if it was the first.

"Idiotic whore! Imbecile!" He screamed. He kicked and kicked and I screamed and screamed. I screamed for help, not that I thought anyone would hear me.

But I had to do something, so I screamed.

Finally, he stopped, walked away, and left me on the floor in a crumpled, bloody mess. I was relieved. I thought he was finished, so I tried to pull myself together. I tried to stand up, but it was difficult for me to even sit up, let alone stand. My face was a mess of tears and snot, and as I wiped at it with my hand, I could feel the lingering sting in my jaw.

I was still on the floor when he returned. My eyes were closed as I lay there, but I felt and heard his footsteps thud against the wooden floor. I opened my eyes to find him standing over me, glaring at me. He had more rage to share with me. I was sure of it. I could see it in *his eyes. He lifted his hand in which he held a necktie. He squatted down beside me and wiped my face with the tie. He rubbed his hand across my hair and whispered, "Truly a beauty never beheld before. Such sweet innocence she invokes. Such serenity surrounds her being." He smiled at me as he finished an excerpt from Ode to Olivia. He leaned over and kissed me softly on the lips. Maybe he's done, I thought.*

*But then he gagged me with the tie.*

*My eyes widened and I whimpered against the gag as he began to kick me again. I screamed and cried into the gag, trying to beg him to stop. My screams became dry heaves as I fought to breathe through the gag.*

*He kicked and punched me in the stomach and between my legs for a long while, until he was satisfied that he'd gotten rid of the baby, as he put it. I lost consciousness several times throughout the ordeal. I'd awaken to more blows, more screaming insults from David, and then I'd pass out again. The final time I came to, he was dragging me, literally dragging me up the stairs to our bedroom. He put me on the bed and had his way with me. I was bleeding, and in so much pain, but he didn't care. He only cared about fulfilling his own needs at that moment.*

*I was sore for weeks after that and at first, I could barely walk. I had a couple of bruised ribs. I hid my facial bruises from Jason by wearing a thick coat of make-up. About a month later, David took me to the doctor to have my tubes tied. I remember that doctor's visit well because it was the first real physical exam I'd had since Jason was born. I remember sitting in the doctor's office and listening to him tell me that I had gonorrhea and how we'd both need to be treated for it. David was in the office with me. Once we left the doctor's office and were on our way home, David started laughing.*

*"What's funny," I asked, cautiously. Anything I said, no matter how innocent, was liable to set him off.*

*"I was kind of hoping we'd have HIV. That would make for a good book, huh? But who knows what the future holds, my darling. Right?" I didn't answer him. I just turned and stared out of the car window and wondered if things would ever get any better...*

"Dear Lord," Ben said. "Olivia, I've got to know. Why didn't you just take Jason and leave him?"

"There were several reasons. He was always threatening to harm Jason or himself, and he also threatened to show the video tapes to a lawyer and sue me for custody of Jason if I left. He said he'd win because the tapes proved I was an unfit mother. I couldn't take a chance on him raising my child. David was...he was sick."

"*That* he definitely was."

I nodded. "I hope that you never know what it feels like to be treated like that, Ben."

Ben shook his head. "Olivia, I…"

"It's okay. From then on, he made sure the men used condoms, plus my tubes were tied, so there was no way I'd get pregnant again."

"*From then on?* Good Lord. You mean he kept bringing men home?" He asked with wide eyes.

"Not exactly. Um…can we stop here? I'm worn out."

"Of course. Let me walk you home."

Ben walked me to Jason's door and kissed my forehead. "How about we break for a few days? I know this is emotionally taxing on you."

I smiled. "Thanks."

I walked into the apartment to find Jason asleep on the sofa. I covered him with a blanket and thanked God I didn't have to face him after what I'd just revealed to Ben.

## *Twelve*

## "So Amazing"

*Early* Sunday morning, I was awakened by Jason. I peered at him through drowsy eyes and almost instantly panicked. "W…what day is it?" I asked as I tried to sit up, my feet caught in the covers.

Jason placed his hand on my shoulder and shook his head. "No, it's alright. It's Sunday."

I breathed a sigh of relief. "What's going on?"

"Everything's okay. Ben's invited us to church this morning."

"Church?"

"Yes. I've been to his church a couple of times. It's nice. I'm going to church with Sandra, but you're welcome to go with Ben if you want to."

I smiled. "Sandra? Sounds like things are getting serious. When do I get to meet her?"

Jason returned my smile. "Soon, I promise."

"I can't wait."

"What do you want me to tell Ben? He's waiting at the door."

"Oh. Well, tell him I'll pass."

Jason nodded. "Okay."

I lay back in the bed and a few minutes later, Jason left for Sunday school at Sandra's church. I'd almost drifted back off to sleep when I heard a knock at the front door. I wrapped the quilt around my body and drug myself to the door. On the other side stood Bennett Paul, looking like a page from a men's fashion magazine. His dark skin contrasted with the cream colored suit he wore. For a moment, I thought I was dreaming. Could a human being really look that good? I stood with my mouth hung open and tried to find at least one word to say, but I couldn't. I was totally and completely speechless.

"I won't take 'no' for an answer," he said softly.

"Uh, b...but I have nothing to wear. Look at you! You look like you're going to a formal affair." He stepped closer to me and I could smell his aftershave. He placed his hands on my shoulders and I think I felt sparks travel down my arms.

"You don't have one little dress? Not one?"

I'm a mature woman, so of course I had brought a dress. I knew not to travel unprepared, but Ben's nearness was unnerving and I couldn't answer him. Ben was one gorgeous man.

"Okay, if you don't have a dress, I'll just have to go out and buy you one. What size?"

His last statement broke the spell. I laughed. "I'm not telling you my size."

"Then will you do me the honor of changing clothes and accompanying me to church?" He leaned over and kissed my cheek. "Please?"

I closed my eyes and shook my head. *He definitely knows how to get what he wants.* "Fine, I'll go with you."

~*~

I couldn't remember the last time I'd stepped foot in a church. It had to be before my grandmother passed. Bevvie never missed a Sunday or a Wednesday in church and she never allowed me to miss, either.

I looked down at my knee-length black dress and felt out of place. It was more than appropriate for a dinner party or an evening out on the town, but it was not necessarily a "church dress". I sighed. It was all I'd brought with me so I'd just have to deal with it. Hearing my sigh, Ben squeezed my hand and smiled down at me. It was an adequate expression of reassurance.

Ben's church was located on the south side of Chicago. It was small and the pews were packed. Everyone greeted me with a smile and seemed genuinely glad to meet me. I soon found out that Ben's cream suit was actually an usher's uniform. Throughout the service, he manned the main sanctuary entry doors. I sat near him at the rear of the church.

The choir was small but powerful. I closed my eyes and smiled as they sang. I didn't usually listen to gospel music, but I felt them singing from their hearts about how they just couldn't stop praising God's name. I absorbed their sincerity. It was such a nice feeling.

The pastor, Reverend Collins, was an enthralling preacher. He captured and kept my attention from the moment he stepped into the pulpit and began to speak. He was a short, compact, medium brown-skinned man with a booming voice. I noticed many of the churchgoers jotting down notes as he spoke from Jeremiah 29:11. "God has great plans for you," he said. "No matter your age or your circumstances, He still has a great work to do in your life." As he spoke, I wondered if what he said was true for me. At forty-two and with so little education, what could God possibly have in store for me? For my future?

Once the service had ended, I stood by as Ben fellowshipped with some of the members. I was thankful that he introduced me only as Olivia, leaving the Moy off. "Moy" was too easily recognizable, and I was in no mood to hear people gush about David's brilliance, even if it was the truth.

We had lunch that afternoon at Saltillo's, a small soul food restaurant. There I shamelessly enjoyed fried pork chops, collard greens, black-eyed peas, and cornbread. I washed it all down with a tall glass of sweet tea. I enjoyed the food, the family atmosphere, and of course, Ben's company.

On the way back home, Ben smiled over at me and asked, "Have you enjoyed your day so far?"

I nodded. "It's been wonderful. Thank you for inviting me."

"Been a while since you attended church?"

"Years. David didn't like going to church. He said he loved God, but he didn't like churches or the people in them."

"So, David made all of the decisions? Even when it pertained to religion?"

I sighed. "For a long time, he did." I paused and then asked, "Ben, do you think God will forgive me for all the things I've done? The bad things I did for David?"

Ben glanced at me and nodded. "I know He will, Olivia. I know that for sure. All you have to do is ask Him. He'll forgive you of anything you've done. He loves you."

I looked down at my hands clasped in my lap. "*Anything?*"

"Yes, *anything* and *everything*."

I smiled and turned towards the passenger-side window.

"You know what I want?" Ben asked.

"What?"

"I want for us to have a David Moy-free day, today."

I looked over at him. "Okay. What do you want to do?"

Ben parked his Honda Accord in front of his building and then turned towards me. "I want you to go change into something more comfortable and meet me at my place for a relaxing afternoon."

I laughed. "Doing what?"

"You'll see."

About thirty minutes later, I sat next to Ben on his overstuffed sofa and smiled. Our relaxing afternoon consisted of buttery popcorn, orange sodas, vanilla ice cream, and old movies. I knew he'd been a student of African American cinema and theater, but I had no idea how extensive his DVD collection was. I browsed through the cases, and finally settled on *The Bronze Venus* and *Stormy Weather*. I'd always loved the beautiful Lena Horne. In all those years that my life was consumed by David, I'd almost forgotten that.

Ben was good at giving me little historical nuggets throughout the movies. He knew who'd written the music, where the films were shot, and even the names of some of the extras. I thoroughly enjoyed his commentary.

The evening began to wind down and as the ending credits of *Stormy Weather* scrolled down the screen, Ben turned to me and took my hand in his. "Olivia, there's something I need to tell you. I don't know if this is the appropriate time, but I need to say it."

I nodded. "Okay."

"When I hear about the things you've been through, the pain you've endured, it breaks my heart. It really does. Olivia, you are so strong and so brave. Jason is a very lucky young man to have a mother who literally sacrificed her life for him."

I looked down at our joined hands. "I...I only did what I felt I had to do."

He nodded. "I know. Olivia...I care about you. And I want to help you to heal."

I looked him in the eye. "You *are* helping me. Talking about the past, sharing my experiences with you, that's helping me to heal. It hasn't been easy to do, but more and more I can feel the weight being lifted off of me. Thank you."

"I'm glad to hear that, because I have some selfish reasons for wanting you to heal."

I frowned. "What do you mean?"

He caressed my cheek and smiled. "I'm falling for you. I want to be with you."

"What?"

He leaned in and kissed me softly on the lips. "I want to be with you, Olivia. I am very attracted to you—not just physically, either. I want all of you, especially your heart."

I felt tears well up in my eyes. His words were overwhelming. "Ben...I..."

He placed his finger to my lips. "Shh. I understand that you need time and I'll give it to you." He kissed me again. I wrapped my arms around his neck and kissed him back. He held me closely and I felt so safe with him. For the first time in many years, I felt completely safe with a man.

"There's something I need to tell you about me. Something you need to know," he said.

I looked up at him and saw the nervous look on his face. "W…what is it?"

He sighed as he released me and slumped against the back of the sofa. "It's about my past…my marriage. I haven't been totally truthful about things."

I frowned. "What do you mean?"

"Olivia…the reason I'm not in my son's life is because I can't be."

"What? What does that mean?" He was beginning to frighten me.

"Olivia, I abused his mother. I…I used to hit her."

My eyes fell to the floor as I tried to get a handle on what he was saying. "I don't understand. You…you what?"

"I…I hit her two times. Once right after we were married. The second time I hit her, I broke her jaw…and she left me. There's a restraining order. I can't go near her. I can only visit my son in public places and under supervision. It was just too embarrassing, and I was ashamed of what I'd done and who I was, so I moved away."

How could this be true? Ben, a batterer? *Is this the only kind of man I can attract?* "Why? Why did you hit her?"

He shook his head. "I don't have an excuse other than the fact that my father abused my mother. He never hit us kids, just like I never hit my son, but he would abuse my mother. It was horrible and I vowed I'd never be like him. Sometimes, we become what we know, what we grow up seeing, despite our best efforts not to. I hate myself for how I treated her. I hate the man I was back then," he said, his voice breaking.

I stared at him. I was speechless and heart-broken.

"I'm not using my upbringing as an excuse. But its how I was back then."

I could feel a tightness forming around my head, as if someone was squeezing my brain. "You're not like that now?"

He shook his head and with a desperate look in his eyes said, "No, I'm not. I prayed and I worked hard to become a different man. I am a different man. I'd never ever hurt another woman." He placed his hand on my cheek. "I would never hurt you. I promise."

I frowned and looked away. "Ben, I don't know how you can promise something like that. I don't know how I can believe you after what I've been through."

"Please, give me a chance. I told you because I thought you needed to know. But I don't want to lose you. It was my past, Olivia.

I've changed."

I stood from the sofa. "I think I should go now. I…" I looked around the room, my eyes searching for something and nothing in particular. I was confused to say the least. Confused and disappointed.

Ben stood next to me and laid his hand on my arm. I flinched. All of the safety he'd represented to me had disappeared. He was a threat to me now. He was David.

"Olivia—"

I shook my head as my tears began to stream down my cheeks. "Ben, I'm sorry, but I can't." With that, I left his apartment and crossed the hall to Jason's, my heart breaking into a million pieces.

~*~

I spent the next few days holed up in Jason's apartment, trying to nurse my broken heart. Trying to make sense of what Ben had told me. How could it be? How could Ben be an abuser? I saw no signs. In his eyes I only saw goodness. Could I really be that blind? Was I really that naïve?

I sat in the living room and stared at the door. I wished I could see through it. I wished I could see all the way through it to Ben's living room, to Ben. I missed him terribly. Maybe, just maybe I was falling for him. He said he'd changed. He said he was a different man now. Maybe he was. I wanted and needed him to be a changed man. I needed him. I needed him *desperately*.

Besides, who was I to judge his past after what I'd revealed to him? He wanted me knowing my past. *He still wanted me.* That had to count for something.

I grabbed a pen and a piece of paper from the coffee table. On it I wrote:

*We need to talk. – Olivia*

I decided I'd slip it under his door so that when he returned home from work, he'd find it. I quickly walked across the hall and slid the paper underneath his door. Before I could take one step back towards Jason's door, Ben's door swung open. I turned around to see Ben standing there in nothing but his plaid boxers, a forlorn look on his face, the note in his hand.

"I…I thought you were at work," I stammered.

"I should be. I'm not feeling all that well," he replied.

"Oh."

"Do…do you want to come in," he asked softly—apprehensively.

I nodded and walked into his familiar home. We sat across from each other in silence for several minutes before I finally found the right words and spoke them.

"I was wrong to leave the other day. I…I was afraid," I confessed.

Ben dropped his eyes. "I'm sorry. I'm so sorry for my past, Olivia. I wish I could erase it, but I can't. But I assure you that I am nothing like that now. I would never ever lay a hand on you."

I sighed. "Can I ask you something?"

"Anything."

"When you hit your wife, how did you feel?"

He frowned slightly. "What?"

"What did it feel like to hit her? Did you feel good? Powerful?"

"Olivia, I—"

"I need to know. I need to know what goes through a man's mind when he abuses someone he loves. *I need to know*," I said anxiously.

Ben slumped against the back of his seat, his eyes downcast. "For a brief moment, I felt powerful, I guess. But that feeling was quickly replaced by a heavy feeling of self-loathing. I hated myself for hurting her. I hated myself for being what I never wanted to become. I hated myself for a long time, but then God forgave me, and I forgave myself."

I nodded, and a silence settled between us again. I closed my eyes and sighed. What was I to do?

"Olivia," Ben said, "I really struggled with the idea of telling you about my past. I could've kept this from you, but I knew it was right to tell you. I also knew that by telling you, I was taking a chance on losing you. I don't want to lose you. If you give me a chance, I will show you that I've changed. If I ever lay a hand on you, I will cut it off myself. I mean it."

I stared at him for a moment and then said, "If after all I've told you about me, you haven't judged me, I have no right to judge you. The Ben Paul I know is kind and gentle. If you say you've changed, then I believe you."

Ben closed his eyes and smiled. "Thank you. Thank you for giving me a chance, for giving us a chance. You will not regret it. I promise."

He crossed the room and took me into his arms. I rested against his body and hoped I'd made the right choice.

## *Thirteen*

## "The Night I Fell In Love"

*I* was the first to hear the knocks at the door. Ben and I had fallen asleep on his sofa after a night of marathon movie-watching, and the sunlight peaking in through the curtains told me that a new day had dawned. I sat up on the sofa and shook Ben until he'd awakened. He sat up and smiled at me. "What is it, beautiful?"

I couldn't help but to return his smile. "Someone is at your door."

He kissed me on the cheek and left to answer the door. I smoothed the front of my t-shirt and rubbed my hand over my hair. I usually wouldn't have relished the thought of spending the night on a couch, but there in Ben's arms, I'd had the sweetest sleep I can remember.

Ben opened the door and on the other side stood Jason with a panicked look on his face. I'd forgotten all about Jason.

"Have you seen my mother? I've been calling her but she left her phone at my place." Before Ben could answer, Jason looked past him and saw me. "Mother!" He rushed past Ben into the room. His pale brown skin was flushed. His eyes read relief. "I was worried sick! What are you still doing over here?"

"Uh, we were watching movies and I fell asleep."

Jason looked over at Ben, who remained silent, then he looked back at me. "Well, I'm leaving for work now. Don't ever scare me like that again!"

"I...I'm sorry, Jason," I said softly.

He returned his attention to Ben. "Dr. Paul, are you off today?"

Ben shoved his hands into the hip pockets of his jeans. "Actually, I am."

Jason nodded. "Well, I've left the door open for you, Mother. I'll see you this evening."

"Okay. Have a good day, son." I watched him leave and then shook my head. "I didn't realize we'd slept the night away."

Ben moved closer to me. "I'm sorry. I should have taken you home." He sat down beside me and kissed me. "But it felt good having you here."

I kissed his cheek. "It felt good to be here. But whatever's going on between us, I can't tell Jason about it yet. I don't think he's ready."

Ben nodded. "I know he's not."

I stood from the sofa. "I should go now. Enjoy your day."

"The only way I'll be able to do that is if you spend it with me."

I looked down at him. "Ben, maybe we should slow down."

Ben stood up next to me and placed his hands on my arms. "Actually, I thought we were moving pretty slowly already."

"I…I just don't want to do anything to upset Jason."

Ben looked at me with such affection; I found my eyes locked with his. "Jason's an adult, a very intelligent man. It's your time now, Olivia. It's your time to be happy, and if you'll let me, I believe that I can make you happy."

I cupped his face with my hands. "You already do."

"Then don't stop me."

I sighed. "Ben…"

"I'm not asking you for your hand in marriage. I just want to spend some time getting to know you. What's your maiden name?"

"LaVeaux. That's where David got Ella's name. Ella was my mother's first name."

He nodded. "I want to get to know Olivia LaVeaux. What she

likes, what she dislikes. I want to know everything about her."

I shook my head. "She's been gone for a long time."

He pulled me into a hug. "Then let me help you find her."

I rested my head on his chest. "Okay."

~*~

We spent the day driving around the city. Ben showed me anything and everything that Chicago had to offer. We had lunch at a small restaurant near the apartment building and I must say that I could've eaten three or four of those Italian beef sandwiches. They were delicious!

We ended our day back at his apartment in front of the TV. I finally got to watch Jason's copy of *Imitation of Life*. Ben held me as I cried at the movie's ending. It was a good day.

## Fourteen

## "Sometimes It's Only Love"

*I* hummed as I flipped the pancakes in the skillet, and I smiled as Jason walked into the kitchen and took a seat at the table. "Good morning. You're up early," he said.

"I wanted you to have a good meal before you went to work. And I wanted to talk to you about something."

"Okay."

I sat the plate of smoked links, fried eggs, and pancakes in front of him and then sat across from him at the table.

"Wow, thanks, Mother! This looks delicious," he said as he dug into his breakfast.

"Anything for you."

"So, what did you want to talk about?" he asked between bites of food.

"I really have enjoyed my stay, but you're an adult and I realize that you need your privacy. I think it's time for me to leave."

Jason looked up from his plate, an expression of concern on his face. "Mother, you don't have to leave. I love having you here."

"I love being here. I was thinking that maybe I could get a place here in Chicago and lock up the house back in Arkansas or maybe we could sell it."

"Sell it? But I thought you wanted to keep it because Father loved it so much," he sounded a little upset.

"Well, we don't have to sell it. Like I said, we could just lock it up for now. I…I'd just rather not go back there…"

Jason nodded. "Oh…okay. Do you want me to take you house hunting?"

"Um, actually, Ben says the tenants in the apartment directly below his are moving out at the end of the week. I was thinking about leasing it."

He frowned and laid his fork down on the table. "Really? I don't know, Mother. This neighborhood is not the best."

"If it's good enough for you, it's good enough for me."

He shrugged. "Well, at least you'll be close and that way you and Ben can complete the book."

I nodded. "I won't crowd in on your life. I'll just be in my little apartment alone."

"Oh Mother, you could never crowd in on my life. You are the best mother in the world and I mean that. You know, I'm glad that you and Ben are friends. I hope you'll make more friends."

"I do, too."

~*~

Ben and I laughed and talked as we painted the living room walls of my new apartment. We'd been cleaning and painting it little by little for two weeks and it was the most fun I'd had in years. I was growing to care for Bennett Paul more and more. I liked being with him, and I trusted him implicitly.

We worked and worked until finally taking a break to eat lunch. It was a Saturday and we were almost finished fixing up the entire apartment. I was excited about moving in and I was even more excited about making a new start.

"Thanks for helping me," Ben said. "I'll have to knock this off of your rent."

I crossed my legs Indian-style as I sat across from him on the tarp-covered floor and smiled. "I'm enjoying it, and I'm enjoying you."

Ben sat his sandwich down. He leaned over and kissed me. I tasted his pastrami on wheat.

"Mm, what was that for?" I asked.

"Nothing in particular. Are you finding Olivia LaVeaux?"

I nodded. "Yes, I think I am."

"And what have you found out about her so far?"

"Um, let's see. She likes to sleep late. She likes old movies and slow love songs, especially Luther Vandross. She really loves his music. Um, she loves a room full of sunlight. She loves food of all kinds. But, most of all, she loves the company of the handsome Dr. Bennett Paul."

He leaned forward and kissed me again. "I love your company, too."

"I'm glad to know it."

Ben smiled and hopped to his feet. "I'll be right back."

I shrugged. "Okay."

I'd almost finished my roast beef sandwich when he returned with a small boom box in his hand. He sat it on the floor and plugged it into the outlet, then pressed play on the CD player. I looked up at him and smiled as the orchestral music began to play. "Love Won't Let Me Wait" was one of my favorite songs. Ben reached for my hand and pulled me to my feet. He pulled me into his arms and I rested against his body. We danced until the song had ended and then Ben leaned in and kissed me deeply. I wrapped my arms around his neck and savored every second of that kiss.

We slid to the floor and Ben held me tightly as he continued to kiss me. When our kiss ended, he gazed into my eyes and caressed my cheek with the back of his hand. "Can I do something for you right now?" he asked.

I closed my eyes and nodded. He kissed my neck and my body stiffened.

"Do you trust me?" he asked.

With my eyes still closed, I nodded. "I do, but my body is not my own anymore. It's used up. I'm ashamed of it."

Ben kissed my closed eyelids. "Your body is beautiful and it's not used up. It just needs to be loved. Let me show you."

I nodded again and tried to relax. Ben softly kissed my neck again and whispered. "See, that's what love feels like."

I began to relax beneath his touch. He took his time and planted soft, tender kisses up and down my arms, in the crook of my neck, on the small of my back. As I lay there, tears flooded my eyes. I was moved by the shear tenderness of his touch. He blazed a trail of love all over my body and I felt it all the way to the depths of my heart. Bennett Paul loved me and without him even saying it, I felt every ounce of his love.

He worked his way back to my mouth and kissed me for what felt like hours. Then he kissed my wet eyes and held me tightly in his arms.

I lay there next to him for a moment and then whispered, "Ben, I don't do well with intimacy. I…I'm not ready to—"

Ben shook his head. "Shh. I understand. I just want to make you happy. That's all I care about. The rest will come with time. I love you, Olivia."

I rested my head on his chest. It felt good to be loved by him. I wanted to feel his love forever.

## *Fifteen*

## "Too Far Down"

"*Once Her Body's Fire* was published, we moved again. This time to New York. We lived in a nice apartment in Manhattan and I can honestly say that those four years in New York were happy, peaceful years. During that time David wrote two non-fiction books. One was an authorized biography of his favorite African American poet, Charles Dunn Downey. The other chronicled the early history of African American literature," I said.

"Yes, both of those were standards at most HBCUs. I remember them well," Ben said.

I nodded. "At that time, Jason attended a really nice day school and I spent most of my days volunteering there. We always ate dinner together, went on weekend trips as a family. I really treasured those years. David was a wonderful father and husband during that time, and I really thought all of the pain that accompanied the 'Ella' years was behind us."

"But it wasn't?" Ben said.

I shook my head. "No. When Jason was ten, David was awarded an honorary doctorate degree from Morehouse. So we all flew to Atlanta for the ceremony. David was so excited and at first, we had a wonderful time there."

Ben raised his eyebrows. "At first? What happened?"

"Once we made it back to our hotel room that evening after the ceremony, David was furious with me. He sent Jason down to the hotel's pool and then began screaming at me about flirting with some man who was sitting next to me during the ceremony. He said he watched us from the platform. I had no clue what he was talking about. I had spoken to the man beside me and given him a friendly smile, but that was it…"

*"You wanted to sleep with him, didn't you?" David said.*

*I shook my head. "No…of course not."*

*David looked into my eyes. "You miss it? You miss being Ella?"*

*I began to feel anxious. Not this again. "No…no, David. No, I don't miss it. I'm happy with our life. I'm happy with you." I may as well have been talking to myself.*

*He nodded. There was a gleam in his eyes. "That's it. You want to choose your own partners now, don't you? It makes perfect sense. Ella was a woman who controlled her circumstances. You want that control, too."*

*I fell to my knees in front of where he sat on the bed. "No...no, that's not it. Please, David. I don't want to be Ella again. Please..." I pleaded.*

*He smiled and cupped my face in his hands. He kissed me softly on the lips. "Your wish is my command." I was relieved. I definitely did not want that madness to return to our lives.*

*Later that night, after we'd all gone to bed, and I'd drifted off into a peaceful sleep, I was awakened by a slap to my face. I bolted upright in the bed and saw David standing over me with a look of rage on his face. "Get up," he ordered.*

*I held my cheek. "W...what is it? What happened?"*

*"Get dressed. We're going out."*

*"W...where are we going?"*

*He slapped me again and I fell back onto the bed. He leaned over me and grabbed a handful of my hair. "We go where I say we go," he hissed, then kissed me hard, biting my tongue in the process.*

*He let me go and shoved me. I fell back onto the bed covering my mouth with my hand. I glanced over at Jason who was fast asleep on the other queen-sized bed in the room. "What about Jason?" I said with a lisp.*

*"He can stay. We won't be long. Now, enough with the damned*

*questions.* ”

*I nodded and then climbed out of the bed.*

*“Wear something nice,” he said.*

*A few minutes later we were sitting in the back of a taxi and my head was filled with questions I was afraid to ask. I could tell by the look in his eyes that he was in a zone. There was something he wanted to do, and if I stood in his way, he wouldn’t hesitate to plow over me.*

*The cab pulled to a stop at the entrance of a night club and though my curiosity was piqued, I kept my mouth shut and followed David into the dark club. I could feel the pounding of the loud club music in my chest, as if my heart had taken on its rhythm. David led me to a table near the rear of the club and quickly shooed the waitress away. We sat in silence and I could see David surveying the crowd as if he was looking for something or someone. A feeling of dread washed over me as my heart continued to thud in my chest.*

*After we’d been there for about twenty minutes, he said, “Pick one.”*

*I looked over at him and said, “One what?” But I knew what he meant.*

*“A man. Pick a man for tonight.”*

*No...no...no. I shook my head. "No. David, please..."*

*He glared at me and with venom in his voice said, "You embarrassed me today, darling. If you want to be a whore, then you'll be one on my terms. PICK ONE!"*

*A tear trickled down my cheek. "David, I can't do it. I don't want anyone but you. I really don't. Can't you see that?"*

*He leaned across the table and grabbed my hand. He squeezed it so tightly that I nearly screamed. "You will pick a man right now or I will go back to that hotel room and throw your son over the balcony. Keep your promise, Olivia, and I'll keep mine."*

*He let go of my hand and I wiped the tears from my face. I looked around the room and quickly chose a young man whom I would later learn was an Emory student. David smiled and commended me on my choice. "I bet he'll do a wonderful job," he said. He walked over and talked to the young man while I sat at the table fighting the urge to run away. Where would I go? I noticed the young man as he looked over at me and smiled then nodded and shook David's hand.*

*The deal was sealed.*

*We all piled into another cab and rode to a different hotel. I lay in the bed and closed my eyes. I disappeared again. It was the only way I knew how to cope. David watched and every once in a while I'd feel him kiss me or hear him tell me how much he loved me, how sexy I was...how beautiful I was, how much he wanted me. When the young man was finished with me, David took his turn. He asked the young man to stay and watch and then, when David was finished, he gave the young man another turn. It was the next morning before they were done.*

*When we made it back to the room, Jason was still asleep, thank God. We returned to New York the next day and David announced that he'd had such a good time in Atlanta he wanted to move there, permanently. A month later, we did just that.*

Ben shook his head. "I'm sorry, Olivia."

I dropped my eyes. "For what? You are not David."

"I wish I'd known you back then. I wish I could've helped you...or something."

I shrugged. "I doubt if I would've accepted your help. I was afraid of him and afraid of losing him at the same time. He was all I had...he and Jason."

"I can't believe I've never heard about this before. I can't believe none of these men came forward. David was very famous."

I sighed. "David was *paying* them, Ben. He was paying them for their services *and* their silence. Besides, not many of those men even realized who David was. I don't think they were literary buffs."

Ben sighed heavily. "I see. Do you want to stop for now?"

I shook my head. "No, we can go on."

"Okay, well, how was living in Atlanta?"

"The city was nice, but my life there was not."

Ben leaned forward in his chair and grasped my hand. "Why?"

I took a deep breath and released it. "Well, David began working on a new novel. He wanted to try his hand at a different genre of literature."

Ben nodded slowly. "That's when he wrote *Lover's Quarrel*, a suspense thriller."

"Yes and the new genre required new research."

"No more men?"

I laughed bitterly. "Oh, the men were no longer research, they were recreation. We went to a different club every Saturday night, and I was required to choose a different partner, but it was all for fun."

"David's fun?"

I was taken aback. "Certainly not mine!"

Ben stood and walked over to the sofa. He sat down beside me and wrapped his arm around my shoulders. "I didn't mean it that way."

I closed my eyes and sighed. "I know. But can't you see? This is why I don't like being in public. I never know if there will be someone around who remembers me from the past, someone I've been with. There were so many…"

Ben kissed my forehead. "I'm sorry, Olivia."

"It's okay."

"You sure you don't want to stop now?"

I shook my head. "His new research involved him locking himself in his office all day long, reading mystery novels and watching suspense movies. At first I was relieved, but then I began to grow lonely. I thought about getting a part-time job or doing some volunteer work, but when I talked with David about it, he told me I could just be his assistant. It was my job to go to the library or book store or video rental store every day.

"I became a regular at the video rental place. One of the clerks was very friendly, and we'd always have a little chat when I dropped in. His name was Kyle, and I thought he was such a nice man. One day, we were alone in the store and he told me he had a couple of movies he'd put back for me. He locked the front doors and alarms went off in my head, but I didn't listen to them. I was too stupid to listen to them."

"You weren't stupid, Olivia."

"Yes, I was…"

*I followed him to the back and he locked the storeroom door behind us. He smiled at me and began to undress. "What are you doing?" I asked.*

*"I've seen you in the clubs. Why won't you choose me?" he asked.*

*I turned to leave and he grabbed the back of my head and shoved my face into the door. It hurt like hell and I literally saw stars. He turned me around and forced his mouth onto mine. I bit his lip as hard as I could, but I was still dazed. He yelped loudly and shoved me to the floor. I hit my head hard, on the concrete, but I didn't lose consciousness. My head throbbed and I couldn't move. I lay on the floor with the taste of his blood in my mouth.*

*I watched as he stood over me naked. He stripped my clothes off of me as I moaned in protest. I couldn't scream or move, but I cried and I moaned as he took me. He held his hand over my mouth and I'll never forget the smell of his sweaty palms, the sounds he made, the look in his eyes. I wanted to fight, but my head hurt so badly. I laid there and endured it and the only thought running through my mind was that I'd made a name for myself in Atlanta. So much so, that this man thought he could just have me, my body, without my consent.*

*When he was done with me, I stumbled to my feet and when he let me leave, I somehow drove back home. As soon as I made it into the house, I knocked on the door to David's study. He opened it and held out his hand without even looking at me. If he'd looked at me, he would've seen the blood on my lips, and the bruised knot on my forehead.*

*"Did you get the movies?" he asked.*

*I shook my head and cried. "No. The man at the store, he…he raped me. He raped me!" I collapsed onto the floor in tears.*

*Without a word, David walked past me. I could hear his heavy footsteps as he bounded through the house, moving from room to room. When he returned, he had a gun in his hand. I didn't even know he owned a gun. He reached for my hand and pulled me to my feet. "Come on," he said.*

*I followed him to the car, and we rode in silence to the video store. I was glad that David believed me. I didn't want him to get into any trouble, but I was glad he cared enough about me to be mad.*

*We arrived at the store and David headed straight to the counter with me trailing in behind him. He smiled and introduced himself to*

*Kyle, whose eyes were wide with fear as David lifted his shirt and showed him the butt of the gun he'd shoved into the front of his pants. "Close the store," David said evenly.*

*Kyle stood and stared at David, then his eyes darted towards the entrance.*

*"If you try to run, I will shoot you in the back, my friend. Don't try me," David said.*

*Kyle quickly announced that the store was closing and after the few customers left, he locked the front doors. David pulled the gun from his pants and pointed it at Kyle. "Let's go to the back. I want to see where you raped my wife."*

*Kyle held his hands up. "Look, I—"*

*"NOW!"*

*Kyle trembled as he led us to the storage room. David kept the gun trained on him and calmly said, "Did you enjoy my wife?"*

*Kyle's eyes widened. "Look man, I—"*

*"DID YOU?!"*

*Kyle hesitantly nodded, eying the gun.*

*David smiled and then reached over and rubbed my arm. "She's good, isn't she?"*

*Kyle glanced at me but his eyes never left the gun for more than a second. He nodded again.*

*David kept his eyes and the gun on Kyle as he kissed me and then said, "Show me what you did to her."*

*"What?!" Kyle and I said simultaneously.*

*David put the gun to Kyle's temple, forcing the metal against his skin. "SHOW ME OR I WILL BLOW THE TOP OF YOUR HEAD OFF!"*

*Kyle stared at me with an almost apologetic look on his face. Imagine that. My rapist felt sorry for me. "I...I don't know if I can do it under pressure like this," Kyle stammered.*

*"You will do it if you want to live," David said, pressing the gun harder against Kyle's temple.*

*Kyle stared at me and then squeezed his eyes shut as if trying to will himself to do it.*

*"NOW!" David shouted. "NOW! DO IT NOW!"*

*I cried as Kyle yanked down his pants and shoved me to the floor again. David just stood there and watched us with a satisfied look on his face. I closed my eyes and I wished I was dead. It seemed like death would be the only way out of this life...this torture.*

*When Kyle was done, David thanked him. We headed out of the store and once inside the car, David said, "Do you have my movies?"*

*I shook my head and wiped the tears that continued to fall.*

*"Well, go back in there and get them."*

*"What? Please don't make me go back in there, David. Pleeease." He just stared at me and I knew if I didn't comply, I'd pay for it when we got home. I climbed out of that car and was full of humiliation as I headed back into that store and up to the counter. I never took my eyes off of the floor as I asked for David's movies. I paid for them and left in tears. When we made it back home, David showed me how turned-on he was by what he'd witnessed...*

Ben stared at me with tears in his eyes. "Olivia..."

I shook my head and placed my finger to his lips. "It's okay."

He hugged me tightly. "I'm so sorry. I don't understand why he did those things to you."

"He was obviously mentally ill, and by then, so was I."

Ben shook his head. "Don't say that."

"But I really was. I was so depressed after that day, it was all I could do to drag myself out of bed in the morning and get Jason ready for school. It finally clicked in my head that I was nothing

more than a piece of property to David. I was so hurt and so sad, I
forgot about protecting Jason or trying to please David. I couldn't
eat. I spent most of my time in the bed, but I couldn't sleep. I just
wanted to die. That was all I wanted."

A tear rolled down Ben's cheek and I wiped it away. "H…how
did David react to your depression?" Ben asked.

"He ignored me. He didn't really seem to care at all. He was still
engrossed in writing his book. So one day, I wrote a letter to Jason
and after David left to take him to school, I laid it on his pillow. I
took a handful of David's sleeping pills and lay down on the floor
next to Jason's bed. I woke up a couple of days later in the hospital.
It seems that David was paying closer attention to me than I thought.
He'd found me and the note and had rushed me to the hospital."

Ben's brow furrowed. "You…you tried to kill yourself?"

I turned and stared at the wall. "Yes. I just wanted out."

"Dear Lord…"

I shrugged. "It's okay. It ended up being a blessing in disguise."

"How?"

"I finally had the courage to leave him and I told him as much. I
told him that I was taking Jason and that we weren't coming back. If
I was to live, it would have to be without David in my life."

"What did he say?"

"He cried and begged me to stay. He promised that things would change."

"Did they?"

"Yes."

Ben turned the recorder off and grasped my hand. "Good. Enough for now. I love you, Olivia."

I leaned against him. "I love you, too, Ben."

## Sixteen

### "Heaven Knows"

*I* stood in my living room and smiled. I'd bought new furniture and new art for my walls. I was proud of my little place and I was proud of my new beginning. My smile widened as Ben walked from the kitchen into the living room with two glasses of wine. We sat on my sofa and listened to the Luther CD he'd given me as a housewarming gift. As Luther explained to us why a house is not a home, Ben held my hand tightly in his.

"I need to go back to Arkansas to pick up some things," I said softly.

Ben gave me a concerned look. "Are you sure you can do that? Are you ready to go back there?"

I nodded. "I think so. I guess I'm as ready as I'll ever be."

"Then I'll go with you."

I shook my head. "I couldn't ask you to do that. My home holds a lot of memories."

"And that's exactly why I can't let you do this alone. I won't take 'no' for an answer, Olivia. We can travel together or I'll just follow you there, but either way, I'm going."

I looked him in the eye and stroked his cheek. "I just don't understand you sometimes. What could you possibly gain from being so good to me?"

He smiled. "*You.* You're the prize I'm trying to win. Will you let me go with you?"

I shrugged, and with a sigh, said, "Okay."

~*~

We arrived at my house in Arkansas to find it undisturbed, with the exception of the dust which had accumulated on the shelves. I picked the mail up from my neighbor and thanked her for watching the house. When I returned to my house, Ben was standing in front of the fireplace looking at the photos on the mantle.

I stepped behind him and wrapped my arms around his waist. He turned around and pulled me into his arms. "To look at those photos, one would think you two had a perfect life."

I closed my eyes as I rested against him. "Hmm, it took a lot of hard work to keep up that façade."

He turned back around and picked up one of the photos. It was one of David and I dressed to the nines and smiling brightly. "When was this one taken," Ben asked.

"A few weeks before he died. We were at a benefit."

"You looked happy."

"That night, we *were* happy."

Ben nodded as he replaced the photo. He rubbed his hands together. "Where do we start?"

"The bedroom. I have a lot of clothes I need to take back to Chicago."

"Lead the way."

We spent most of the day packing my clothes, jewelry, and a few other items that were to be shipped to Chicago. As I sat on the floor and addressed the boxes, Ben milled around the bedroom. "Where does this door go?" he asked.

I looked up and panic attacked my senses. "That…that's David's closet," I stammered. "Don't go in there! That's where…"

Ben's eyes widened. "Oh…I'm sorry." He walked over to me and crouched down beside me. He looked me in the eye and placed his hand on my shoulder. "I'm sorry...I didn't realize..."

I sighed and laid the black marker down. "It's okay. It's just...I haven't been in there since..."

Ben nodded. "Hey, why don't we go downstairs and wait for dinner? The pizza I ordered should be here soon."

"Okay, you go ahead. Let me finish addressing this last box and then I'll be right there."

He leaned over and kissed my forehead, and I watched as he left the room. I held the marker in my hand, but my eyes were glued to the closet door.

The closet door.

*The closet.*

I stood to my feet and closed the bedroom door. Then I walked across the room to David's closet. I opened the door and stared at the blood stain that remained engrained in the wood of the floor. Try as I had, I never could get that blood stain to disappear. I closed my eyes and heard the gun go off. I heard the gun fall to the floor with a sickening thud. I heard my own shrill screams. The scent of gun powder permeated my nose. I saw the blood as it flowed from David's head. I stared into his open eyes...his beautiful brown blank eyes...and then darkness surrounded me.

~*~

"Olivia! Olivia! Are you okay?" The voice echoed in my head. "Olivia! Oh God, Olivia!"

I slowly opened my eyes and saw a fuzzy form hovering over me. As Ben's face came into focus, I could see that his eyes were full of worry. He lifted me from the bed and held me close to him. "Thank God! Thank God you're alright! You scared me, sweetheart!"

"Wh...what happened?"

"I waited for you downstairs. The pizza arrived and you still hadn't come down, so I came up here to check on you. You were on the closet floor, unconscious. I picked you up and laid you on the bed. I was just about to call 911—"

I jerked away from Ben and in a quick, uncoordinated move stood from the bed. "I was on the floor *in there*?! *The blood...*" I feverishly began to shed my clothes and nearly fell again.

"Olivia—"

"Is...is his blood on me?! Is it on me anywhere?!" My legs were wobbly as I rushed to the mirror in my underwear and tried to inspect my body. The tears flooding my eyes blurred my vision.

Ben moved close to me and placed his hand softly on my back. I flinched. "Olivia," he said softly, "Olivia, there's no blood on you. The blood is dry."

I shook my head as I vigorously rubbed my arms. "I can't have his blood on me…I can't…I can't…"

Ben cupped my face in his hands. "Olivia, there's no blood." He pulled me to him. "No blood, okay?"

I buried my face in his chest and sobbed. "I need a bath. I need a bath right now!"

"Olivia, there's no—"

I pulled away from him. "A bath! I need a bath!" I stumbled as I quickly made my way to the bathroom and shut the door behind me. I could hear Ben's footsteps as he followed me. I began running bath water. I trembled as I stripped out of my underwear. There was a knock at the door. "Olivia?" Ben said softly.

I continued to sob as I lowered myself into the tub and began to scrub my skin. I did not answer him.

"Olivia, are you ok?"

I continued to scrub and cry. The bathroom door slowly creaked open and I looked up at Ben as he cautiously approached me.

Ben walked over to the tub and crouched down beside me. "Let me help you," he said.

I shook my head and continued to scrub.

"Sweetheart, your skin…you're scrubbing too hard. Please let me help you."

I stopped scrubbing and looked down at my arms. They burned like fire. I handed the washcloth to Ben and he dipped it in the water. He jerked his hand back and said, "This water is too hot. You're scalding yourself." He reached towards the faucet but I grabbed his hand.

"No," I said softly.

Ben grasped my hand. "Olivia, let me add some cold water. Just a little."

I looked up at him. "*No.*"

He sighed. "Ok." He rolled his shirt sleeve up and began to gently wash my body as I cried.

I cried.

I moaned.

I screamed.

All the while, Ben continued to wash me and calmly told me that everything would be alright. When he was done washing me, he climbed into the tub, fully dressed, and held me until my tears had ended…until my moans were quieted…until my screams left me hoarse.

~*~

We were sitting in my dining room, eating the cold pizza in silence. I was embarrassed and angry with myself for even opening the closet door, ashamed of how I'd behaved in Ben's presence. *He must really think I'm out of my mind. Maybe I am…*

"Olivia, can I ask you a question?" he asked, interrupting my self-chastisement.

I looked up at him. "Of course."

"Why did you open that door? That was a traumatic experience for you, so why would you want to go in there?"

I sighed as I wiped my hands with a napkin. "Ben, there's something I need to tell you."

He wore a confused expression as he said, "Okay…"

I leaned back in my chair. "The last eight or nine years of my marriage were pretty peaceful. No more men. No more abuse, only the occasional argument, like a regular, ordinary couple."

"Thank God for that," Ben said.

I continued, "But throughout those years, David would go through bouts of deep depression. He wrote and published a couple of books, but he never saw the success he'd seen in the past. He was very unhappy most of the time. The weeks before he died, he would barely get out of bed. Nothing I did would bring him out of his depression."

Ben shook his head. "It wasn't your fault, Olivia."

I closed my eyes. "Ben, please just listen."

He nodded.

I took a deep breath and released it. "The morning it happened…the day he died, he'd perked up. When he woke up, he was actually smiling. We were intimate and it was like when we were young, before the madness began. I was so happy. I thought maybe things were really improving; maybe everything would be alright…"

*David came downstairs where I was cooking breakfast and wrapped his arms around my waist. He kissed my neck. "Come upstairs with me, darling," he whispered.*

*I smiled as I turned the stove off. David took my hand and led me upstairs. "I want to show you something, Olivia," he said.*

*He led me into our bedroom, to his closet, and opened the door. He pulled a box out and sat it on our bed. He opened it and I saw that it was packed full of video tapes. They were each labeled "Ella" with different dates written on them. I was looking upon volumes and volumes of my shame. He pointed to the other boxes in the closet. There were at least ten of them. All of them full of tapes documenting my time with those men. I hadn't realized there were so many. I also hadn't realized that David still had them.*

*With excitement in his eyes, he placed his hands on my arms and said, "I stayed up all night watching these tapes. This is why I'm so happy. Ella makes me happy, darling."*

*I shook my head and backed away from him slowly. Not this again. No, not again.*

*His expression saddened. "I know you don't like being Ella. But it's the only cure for my depression. Don't you see? I need Ella back, darling. I need to relive those glorious days."*

*Amazingly, my eyes were dry as I turned to leave the room. I'd reached the door when I heard the click. "Don't leave," David said softly.*

*Something in his voice made me turn around. He sounded*

*frightened, like a young child whose mother had turned her back on him. I turned around and saw that David had cocked his gun and was holding it to his head. There were tears in his eyes.*

*"If you don't do this for me, I'm as good as dead. I will kill myself before I continue to live in misery, Olivia."*

*I slowly moved towards him. "David, I love you with all of my heart and soul. I want nothing more than to make you happy. But I can't do this. I just cannot go back to that. I'd rather die first. Being Ella is MY misery."*

*He—*

"He killed himself and you feel guilty about it," Ben said, interrupting me. "Sweetheart, it wasn't your fault. David was a sick man and if you ask me, he did you a favor. He freed you."

I shook my head as tears fell from my eyes. "Ben…"

Ben walked around the table to me, lifted my face, and kissed my wet cheeks. "You didn't deserve the things he put you through. He repaid your love for him by humiliating you and facilitating rape over and over again."

I sniffled. "I was only raped once."

Ben shook his head. "No, Olivia. Every time he brought another man into your bedroom, you were raped. You didn't want to have sex with those men. David terrorized you. He *made* you do it. That's rape. He was a damn monster and he got better than he deserved in the end."

I shook my head.

"Olivia, do you miss him?"

I closed my eyes. "Part of me does, simply because I spent most of my life with him. But by and large, no, I don't miss him."

"And you shouldn't. Come on, we'll get a couple of hotel rooms. I don't think it would be a good idea for us to spend the night here."

I nodded. I couldn't argue with that.

Two days later, we'd shipped my boxes to Chicago and left the rest of the house just as it was. We flew back and went straight home. I spent the next few days unpacking the boxes, organizing my place, and trying to leave my past behind me.

*Seventeen*

**"The Best Things In Life Are Free"**

*"Mother*, this is Sandra," Jason said as he walked into my apartment. I smiled and shook the young lady's hand. Sandra was petite, probably only 5'2", and very thin—almost fragile-looking. She had smooth medium brown skin and wide, expressive eyes. Her natural hair was cut close to her scalp. She wore black slacks and a colorful silk blouse. She was absolutely lovely.

"Pleased to meet you, Sandra," I said.

"Thank you. I've heard so much about you, Mrs. Moy. Jason adores you."

"Well, no more than I adore him."

We sat down for dinner and I won rave reviews for my baked ziti. I could see that Jason was truly smitten with Sandra and I was happy for him. I was glad he'd found someone to love. I hoped he'd feel the same for me when I told him about Ben. No, I still hadn't told him, but things between us were getting serious and I knew that eventually I'd have to.

We chatted for a while and I really enjoyed the evening. When I walked Jason and Sandra to the door, I gave Jason a look of approval. He smiled and kissed me goodnight. A few minutes later, Ben arrived at my door. I filled him in on my dinner with Jason and Sandra and we ended up talking until late in the night.

That's how things were with Ben. We could spend hours just talking. He didn't make any demands of me, and he expected nothing from me. To put it plain and simple, he loved me. And I loved him.

~*~

A few weeks later, I smiled at Jason as he sat across the table from me. "Thanks for having breakfast with me," I said.

He nodded as he settled in his seat. "No problem. I've missed you, Mother."

I laughed. "We live in the same building, Jason."

He shrugged. "I miss having you at my place."

I reached across the table and grasped his hand. "Well, you can drop in whenever you like. How are things between you and

Sandra?"

He smiled at the mention of Sandra's name. "Things are going really well. She's a wonderful woman and she's a huge fan of Father's work."

My smile faded as I nodded. "Good. Um…Jason, I need to tell you something."

He took a sip of coffee and said, "Okay…"

"Ben and I have been seeing each other."

Jason swallowed a forkful of scrambled eggs. "So I've gathered." He laid his fork down. "Mother, I don't know how I feel about this."

I sighed. "Well, son, Ben loves me and he's a wonderful man. I love him, too."

Jason stood, walked around the table and squatted down next to me. "Mother, I just want you to be careful. Father's death left you a very wealthy woman. People might want to take advantage of you."

I frowned. "Jason, you've known Ben longer than I have. Surely you don't think he's that type of person. He's been nothing but a gentleman, and he's never asked me for a dime. I have to force him to take my rent payments."

"Just be careful. I worry about you."

I rubbed his cheek gently with my hand. "Don't."

"Easier said than done."

"Well, try. I'll be fine."

He stood up and kissed my cheek. "Okay. How's the book coming along? I can't wait to read it."

"We're almost done. You'll be the first to know."

~*~

I laid my head on Ben's shoulder as we sat on the front stoop of his building and watched the world roll by. I felt such peace when I was with Ben. I never knew that love could be so peaceful.

"I found the Moys," he said softly, shattering my bliss.

I lifted my head and looked at him. "David's parents? Where?"

"Memphis. They live on Avalon Street."

My eyes widened. "Really? That's not far from where we lived when we were there. It's in the historic district, too."

He nodded. "Evidently, they've lived there for more than 40

years. I'm going to see them next week. I think it's important to include his childhood in the book. Maybe they can give some insight as to the adult he became."

I stared out at the passing traffic. "I'll go with you."

"Olivia, I don't think—"

"No. I need to meet them. Maybe then I can understand why he did the things he did. Why he treated me the way he did."

Ben kissed my forehead. "Okay, my love. But I'm not sure if this is a good idea."

"I'll be fine. You and Jason worry too much."

"It's because we love you."

~*~

The Moys lived in a beautiful old two-story home. It's proximity to my old home in Memphis was astounding. Had David chosen a home close to his parents on purpose?

The house was painted stark white and its porch wrapped entirely around it, reminding me of an old plantation house. As Ben parked his rental car on the red-bricked driveway and opened the passenger door for me, I felt my stomach churn. This was David's childhood home, and whatever had occurred inside could possibly explain the pain of my past.

As we walked up to the front door, my nervousness grew. David had told me that his parents didn't approve of me. What if they shut the door in my face? Ben looked down at me and smiled, then rang the doorbell. He gave my hand a reassuring squeeze as we stood there. It was a couple of minutes before a heavy-set white woman opened the door. She smiled at Ben and said, "Dr. Paul, I presume?" Her southern accent was the thickest I'd ever heard.

Ben shook her extended hand and then glanced at me. "Mrs. Moy, this is Olivia, David's widow."

She raised her eyebrows and some of the wrinkles in her face disappeared. With wide eyes she said, "Well, it's nice to finally meet you. You two come right on in."

We followed Jessica Moy into the foyer and her expensive perfume filled our noses. It almost seemed criminal to step on the foyer's shiny mahogany flooring. That foyer was absolutely spotless from the glossy white walls to the sparkling crystal chandelier. A winding staircase with a mahogany banister led upstairs.

I eyed the elegant paintings on the walls as Mrs. Moy led us into the formal living room. She offered us a seat on the burgundy leather

Queen Anne sofa. She sat across from us in a matching chair. Judging from the house and its contents, Mrs. Moy's expensive-looking clothes and pearl jewelry, and the huge rock on her finger, the Moy's were definitely not hurting for money.

I studied Jessica Moy for a moment and tried to see the mother who'd raised David. She must've once been a very beautiful woman. Only that could explain the heavy make-up. She had the appearance of a woman who was holding on for dear life to her youth. I turned my attention to my surroundings. I looked at the many family photos covering the mantel piece, tables, and bookshelves. Several were family portraits of a young Mr. and Mrs. Moy and of David. David bore a striking resemblance to his adopted father. Too striking for them not to be related.

Mrs. Moy's southern drawl broke into my thoughts. "So, Dr. Paul, you're writing a book about our David?"

Ben nodded. "Yes, ma'am. Olivia has been a great help to me, and I've learned a lot about David as an adult. I was hoping to learn about his childhood."

She turned to me. "And Olivia? You are authorizing this book?"

I nodded. "Yes."

She crossed her thick legs and turned her attention back to Ben. "Well, what do you want to know, Dr. Paul?"

Ben pulled his recorder from his jacket pocket and held it up in his hand. "Do you mind?"

Mrs. Moy shrugged in indifference.

Ben switched the recorder on, placed it on his knee, and said, "Will your husband be joining us?"

She clutched her hands in her lap and her expression hardened. "No, I'm afraid Avery is not available."

"Oh, I see," Ben said.

"Well, you'll just have to settle for me," Mrs. Moy said in a huff.

Ben glanced at me. "Alright. How old was David when you and your husband adopted him?"

She sighed and shook her head. "David was not adopted."

"What?" Ben and I said in unison.

"David was my husband's biological child. He was the product of a brief affair Avery had with a local woman. Some little black girl who worked for the law firm—no offense. She was a clerk or secretary or something or other. It happened early in our marriage."

Ben cleared his throat. "Um, so you raised David as your son?"

She nodded and then took her thick hand and fluffed up the back of her long, thin, white mane. "I am unable to have children, so while I was upset about my husband's indiscretions, I saw it as my chance at motherhood—especially when I saw how fair-skinned he was. Why, he could easily pass for a white child."

I sat in stunned silence. Why had David lied?

"Did David know this?" Ben asked.

"Of course. I've read where he said he was adopted, and I think he just wanted to hurt me and his father. It worked." Mrs. Moy replied.

"Why? Why would he want to hurt you?" I asked. *Why did he hurt me?*

"He hated us," she said matter-of-factly.

"Ok, that brings me to this. How was David as a child? What was your relationship with him like?" Ben interjected.

Mrs. Moy sighed and uncrossed her legs, then re-crossed them. "He was quiet and he kept to himself. He was very smart, of course, and an avid reader. At school, when the other children were outside playing, David would stay inside and read."

"Really?" Ben said.

She almost smiled but seemed to think better of it. "Yes. My husband was always so proud of him. He sent him to the best schools and bought him volumes and volumes of books."

Ben nodded. "So he and David had a close relationship?"

She shifted in her seat. "Not really. My husband has always been a very busy man…with his work."

"What kind of work does your husband do?" Ben asked.

"He's a lawyer."

"What about you and David? Did the two of you get along?"

Her expression changed and she turned and stared at the fireplace. "Up until David reached puberty, we got along well enough."

"What changed?"

She shrugged. "*He* changed. He resented the fact that I wasn't his mother, I guess."

"He just changed without cause?" Ben asked, echoing the doubt in my thoughts.

"Yes, he just changed," Mrs. Moy insisted, irritation creeping into her voice.

Ben nodded. "Ok."

She uncrossed her legs and leaned forward in her chair. "Look Dr.

Paul, I was the best mother I knew how to be to him, but he just didn't appreciate it. He grew into a very intelligent, handsome, and virile young man, but he made my life a living hell."

*Virile?* I thought. *What mother describes her child as virile?*

Ben frowned. "How did he make your life a living hell?"

"I was the one who was with him all of the time, and I was basically raising him on my own while Avery worked late into the night. As he reached adolescence, he started to rebel and the closeness we once shared disappeared. He would mouth off at me and he was very disobedient. He'd sneak out of the house at all hours of the night. Avery tried to step in, but David hated him for not being around. Avery got nowhere with David. Plus, David told Avery so many vicious lies about me that he managed to drive a wedge between me and my husband. Our marriage suffered because of that boy."

Ben scooted forward on the sofa. "David was that cunning? He was able to come between you and your husband?"

She laughed. "David Alan Moy was a master manipulator. He was smart, remember? David was thinking when the rest of the world was sleeping. He was a beautiful boy on the outside, but inside, he was full of hate, poisonous hate. He hated me. I'm sure of it."

Ben shook his head. "I don't understand why."

She scoffed, "Neither do I. But I'll tell you this. By the time he was thirteen or fourteen, I couldn't live with him anymore. His behavior and his lies were just too much for me. I was relieved when Avery finally sent him off to boarding school."

"Lies?" I said.

She looked over at me then shifted her eyes. "Yes. He lied all of the time. I don't think David knew how to tell the truth."

"Lies about abuse?" Ben asked.

She crossed her arms at her chest. "Just lies," she said rather curtly.

Ben cut his eyes at me and we exchanged a look that said, *she's the liar.*

Although he knew there was more to what she was saying, Ben moved on. "Was David ever violent?"

"No, but I knew he had the potential to be. I could see it in his eyes."

"Did you or your husband ever try to get him any help?" Ben asked.

Mrs. Moy nodded. "As David grew older, his behavior became

more and more erratic. He'd leave boarding school and show up back here. He'd steal from us, write checks on Avery's account without permission. Then sometimes, he'd be so depressed, he'd lock himself in his room for days at a time. I was not surprised to hear of his death. When he was seventeen, he tried to commit suicide."

Ben looked at me and then said, "How?"

She dropped her gaze to the floor. "He tried to hang himself from the balcony outside his room. Luckily, the gardener saw him. If not, he would've succeeded. It scared Avery half to death. He had him placed in a psychiatric hospital, where David was diagnosed with Bipolar Disorder and started on medication and he was okay for a while. You see, David was your basic tragic mulatto. My daddy always said nothing good would come of mixing the races. David was proof that he was right."

I frowned. *What did she just say?*

David's stepmother continued to speak. "When he decided to go to that college in Arkansas, I knew no good would come of it, but Avery let him go as long as he promised to take his medications, which, of course, he did not do."

Ben glanced at me. "Did David keep in touch after he left for college?"

She stood from her chair and walked over to a window. "For a few weeks he did. Then, some months later, he called and told us that he was married with a baby on the way. We knew he must've been off his medications to be acting so careless. Avery begged him to come home. Told him to bring his wife with him. He just wanted to get him some help. David was very upset with Avery's reaction. He never called us again. We heard nothing more of him until *Prose and Poise* was released." She paused and eyed me for a moment. "His work was beautiful and he certainly adored you, didn't he, Olivia?"

If I didn't know any better, I would've thought I heard a hint of jealousy in her voice. "Yes, he did," I said softly.

She walked back over to her chair and sat down. "It saddened Avery that such genius was contained in such a troubled person. Avery has been mourning David for many years. Since long before he actually died."

We all sat in silence for a moment and then Mrs. Moy turned to me and said, "I don't envy you, young lady. I'm sure that being David's wife was no easy task."

I dropped my eyes and said, "No, it wasn't."

Ben rubbed his hands together. "Um, Mrs. Moy, did you ever see David again after he left for college?"

"Years later, he came to see Avery. He had a young child with him. He didn't want to talk to me, so when he found out that Avery wasn't home, he just turned and left. That was the last we saw or heard from him," she said.

"I see," Ben said.

Mrs. Moy stood to her feet. "Well, it was very nice to meet you both, but I have a lunch date in a few moments."

As it was, she'd dismissed us. She walked us to the door and once we were inside Ben's rental, I settled against the seat and shook my head. "She raised David and she didn't even ask about Jason."

Ben stuck the key in the ignition and looked over at me. "Something's not right about that woman. I can't put my finger on it, but she didn't act like any mother I've met. I have a feeling she was abusive towards David. After all, he was the product of an affair."

I nodded. "I think David's relationship with her has a lot to do with the way he treated me."

Ben started the car. "I guarantee it did."

## *Eighteen*

### "A House Is Not A Home"

"*I* really wish I could get Avery Moy's perspective on things," Ben said as we sat in his suite, eating lunch.

"Me too, but you heard her. He's either unwilling or unavailable to speak with us."

Ben shook his head. "I don't believe Mrs. Moy. She doesn't impress me as being a very forthright person."

"Yeah, I noticed."

Ben sat in deep thought for a moment and then said, "Sweetheart, hand me that phone book. I'm gonna try to reach him at his office."

Sure enough, when Ben called and told Avery Moy's secretary that a Dr. Paul and Olivia Moy were trying to get in touch with him, he not only accepted the call, but quickly invited us to his office to meet with him. A few minutes later, we were on our way to the law offices of Gammel, Arlington, and Moy. After a short wait in the lobby, we were ushered to Mr. Moy's large office.

When I stepped into that office and saw the handsome Avery Moy sitting behind his desk, I was more than taken aback. If I hadn't known any better, I would think I was looking at a ghost. From the deep brown eyes to the thin lips, David Moy had been the spitting image of his father. Honestly, the only difference I could see in them was that David's skin had been slightly darker than his father's. And of course, his father's dark hair was mangled with gray. I found it hard not to stare at him.

Mr. Moy shook our hands and said, "Dr. Paul. Olivia, so good to finally meet you."

I had to force a smile, because the sound of his voice, a voice that perfectly matched David's, was almost too much for me. I managed to keep my composure and answered him with, "It's nice to meet you, Mr. Moy."

He offered us both a seat, and once he'd settled in his chair, said, "So, you two are writing David's biography?"

Ben nodded. "Yes. Olivia has given me a wealth of information about David, and we spoke with your wife this morning. Is there anything you'd like to tell me about your son?"

Mr. Moy's eyes saddened in an instant. "My son…" he said wistfully. He dropped his eyes and shook his head. "I failed that boy. I loved him, but I failed him. I worked all of the time. I left him with my wife, Jessica, and I never should have done that. I don't think she ever got over the fact that he was the child I shared with a mistress."

Ben leaned forward. "Mr. Moy, you don't have to answer this if you don't want to, but, did your wife ever abuse David?"

Avery Moy sighed. "Emotionally? I believe so. I can't be sure though. I wasn't home much."

"Did David ever tell you that she abused him?" I asked.

Mr. Moy closed his eyes and clasped his hands in his lap. There was a period of silence and just as Ben opened his mouth to speak, Mr. Moy said, "Once, when he was about thirteen, just entering puberty, he told me that...that Jessica had touched him inappropriately." He opened his eyes and looked up at us with an expression of shame on his face.

Ben's eyes widened as he glanced knowingly at me. "*Inappropriately?*"

Mr. Moy nodded. "He, uh, said that she did sexual things to him, apparently several times. He had such an active imagination—you can see that in his work. I wasn't sure whether or not to believe him. Months passed and his behavior began to change. He became such a dark person. He was so angry. Jessica started complaining about his behavior, so I sent him off to school. I figured that way, if he was telling the truth, he'd be away from her." His voice broke as he finished his statement.

Ben and I were silent.

Mr. Moy cleared his voice. "I…I was just trying to save my marriage and protect David at the same time. You understand?"

Leaving the question unanswered, Ben said, "Mr. Moy, what do you believe now? Do you believe that David was telling the truth?"

"I know he was telling the truth. Jessica might have told you that he attempted suicide once. But I'm sure she didn't tell you what led up to it." Avery said.

Ben and I sat on the edges of our seats, but remained silent as we awaited Mr. Moy's revelation.

He leaned forward and placed his hands on his desk. I noticed that they were shaking and I could see beads of sweat forming on his creased forehead. He took a shaky hand and rubbed it across his thinning salt-and-pepper hair, then replaced it on the desk. "I made it home from work early one afternoon. Jessica and David were accustomed to me coming home at all hours of the evening, but that day, I decided to come home early. I walked into the house and no one was downstairs, so I figured that they were in their rooms. I walked into my bedroom to find Jessica and David in bed, together. They were…well, you get the idea. All I can remember is dropping my briefcase. When they heard the thud, they stopped and looked at me. David jumped up and ran from the room.

"I followed him into his room and I had it out with him. I was so angry at him. I wasn't thinking straight. I..." He shook his head and cleared his throat. "He told me that she made him do it. That she always made him do it. He told me that she'd even made him have sex with some of her friends as well. He was in tears as he begged me to believe him. I wouldn't listen. I...I yelled at him to stop lying to me. I told him that he was no son of mine and then I left the room. When I went to talk to Jessica, she confirmed what he'd told me. She said she'd been so lonely and that she needed someone. She said that David was so much like me; it felt natural to be with him. *Natural*.

"She actually told me that it wasn't cheating because David was a part of me. She rationalized having sex with a child she'd raised! I thought about the way she'd look at him sometimes, I thought about the signs I'd ignored. I was trying to understand what was going on, trying to make some since of what she'd done, when—"

Mr. Moy turned his back to us and wiped the tears from his face. "The gardener came running in the house. Together, we got David down from the balcony and I resuscitated him and took him to the hospital." He turned back around and faced us. "After that, I did everything I could to help them both. They were both sick and it was my fault. It was my responsibility to take care of them.

"I let David down. Olivia, I know I did. I tried to make it up to him. I tried to reach out to David for years. To apologize. He was my son, my only child, and I loved him."

Another period of silence fell over us as Ben and I digested Mr. Moy's words. My heart ached for David, for the innocent child his parents had corrupted.

After a few more moments, I turned my head towards a bookshelf and said, "Mr. Moy, I respect your pain. I really do. But, you have no idea what you and your wife did to David." I squeezed my eyes shut. "He was a brilliant man, but he was also a tortured soul until the day he died. He shared his pain with my every day of the life we shared together, Mr. Moy. *Every day*." I wiped a single tear from my face and Ben grasped my hand.

Mr. Moy nodded, his own eyes wet with tears. "I haven't slept an entire night in years and when I heard of David's suicide, I fell apart. I left my wife—something I should've done when David was a child. I wish to God I could make things up to David. He would've been better off with his biological mother. I thought I could give him a better life. Jessica is wealthy and I have a good career. I figured we'd be better suited to raise him. I guess I was wrong..."

"Do you still keep in touch with his mother?" Ben asked.

Mr. Moy shook his head. "She passed away some years back. My wife paid her off shortly after David was born and I never heard from her after that. I only learned of her passing after seeing her obituary in the newspaper. Her name was Mary. She was a wonderful woman."

"Is there anything you want to say that we haven't covered?" Ben asked.

Avery Moy closed his eyes and a slight smile crept upon his lips. "I loved my son, and I couldn't have been prouder of his achievements." He turned to me. "Olivia, I'm so very glad to have had the chance to meet you. You are just as lovely as David described you in his poetry. I'd really like to meet Jason, too."

I dropped my eyes to the floor and nodded. "Well, Jason is an adult. If he wants to meet you, he'll contact you."

He nodded. "I understand that. I am truly sorry for David's death."

I looked him in the eye as I said, "So am I."

I sat quietly on the plane next to Ben and thought about David. What I'd learned of him from his parents gave me a new understanding of the man he was. It saddened me to realize that in more than twenty years of marriage, I never knew the real David Moy. I only knew what he wanted me to know of him. As much as he loved me—and I truly believe that he did love me in his own way—he didn't feel he could share that part of his life with me.

The reality of his painful life made his death even more tragic. I leaned on Ben's shoulder as tears flowed freely from my eyes. He wrapped his arm around me and held me tightly. I cried because I loved David so much. I cried because of the pain he endured and then passed on to me. I cried because I finally understood David, but it was too late. I cried because David Moy was dead and for the first time, I wished he was still alive.

## *Nineteen*

## "Love Forgot"

*I* sat nervously in my living room, holding Ben's manuscript in my lap as I waited for Jason to end his phone call. I fingered the edges of the neatly-bound papers and sighed. I'd read the entire book and Ben had done a wonderful job writing it, but I just wasn't sure how Jason would react to it.

Jason finally ended his call and laid his phone down on the coffee table. "Sorry, that was Sandra confirming our dinner plans for tonight."

I nodded. "That's okay."

He smiled. "So, the book is completed? Have you read it?"

I looked at my son for a moment. It felt like it would be my last time seeing him. "Yes, and I want you to read it before it goes to print. But there are some things I want to tell you first. I don't want you to read them in this book. I...I want you to hear them from me."

With a furrowed brow he said, "Okay..."

I closed my eyes and took a deep breath. "Jason, you know that I love you, don't you?"

His frown deepened. "Of course, and I love you. Mother, what is it? What's going on?"

"Honey, there's a lot you don't know about your father. I protected you from many things because I love you so much, but you are an adult now and it's time you knew."

He leaned forward in his chair. "Mother—"

I shook my head. "Let me say this before I lose the nerve."

He nodded, a look of concern shadowing his handsome face.

I blinked back tears. "I know how much you love your father and that you look up to him. I would never want anything to change that." My voice broke as I spoke.

The concern in Jason's eyes deepened. He stood, walked over, and took a seat next to me on the sofa. He grasped my hand. "Mother, what is it? Why are you so upset?"

I rubbed my hand across the top of his. "Jason, your father was a very ill man. He..."

"Father was sick?"

I looked him in his eye. "*Mentally*...he was mentally ill,"

He pulled his hand away from mine. "What are you talking about?"

My tears began to flow freely. "He abused me. For years, he abused and tormented me."

Jason sprung to his feet. "What are you talking about?! Why are you saying this?! You're lying! I never saw him hurt you!"

I looked up at him, my vision blurred with tears. "I am not lying. As much as it hurts to tell you this, it's the truth, Jason. He…he tortured me."

He shook his head as he began to pace the floor. "My father *worshipped* you! He loved you unconditionally! He wrote volumes of poetry for you and this is how you repay him?! By slandering his name? Defiling his memory?"

My heart felt so heavy. "No, Jason. It's the truth."

"It's Bennett Paul, isn't it? He's planted these ideas, these *lies* in your head! He's using you to make a profit and you're letting him! You're the crazy one, not my father!" He snatched the manuscript from me. "This trash will never be published! I will make damn sure of it!" He turned to leave.

I stood from the sofa. "Jason, please listen! *Please* believe me!"

He spun on his heels. The concern in his eyes had completely transformed into anger. "No! *You* listen. Father told me long ago that you were mentally ill. I didn't want to believe him, but now I see that it's true. He told me that you made his life a living hell, but that he'd stayed with you because he loved you. He told me that we had to be sure to take care of you because you're fragile. He loved you so much. How could you do this to him?" His voice wavered.

I walked over to him. I placed my hand on his arm but he snatched away from me. "Jason, I loved your father, too. He will always be the great love of my life, but what I'm telling you is the God's honest truth. *He* was the fragile one, not me. I could not have been fragile and survived what he put me through."

He nodded. "I see now. I see what happened. He tried all those years to make you happy. You are the reason he killed himself. You *drove* him to it!" With that, he stormed out of my apartment with the manuscript in his hand.

I turned and walked back over to my sofa where I curled up into a ball and cried.

~\*~

"*Olivia...Olivia...Olivia...*" The familiar voice repeated my name over and over again. "*Olivia...Olivia...Olivia...*"

I opened my eyes and bolted upright on the sofa. I shook my head as I watched him move closer and closer to me. I squeezed my eyes shut. "You're not real. You're dead," I said softly.

"*Olivia*..." he repeated as he reached for me, his head bloodied, his eyes lifeless.

I shrunk away from him and squeezed my eyes shut again. "No, go away. Go away...go away..."

I sat up on the sofa as the banging at my door awakened me. *It was a dream. It was only a dream.* I sighed with relief and looked around the room as the banging continued. For the first time, I knew without a doubt that I'd been asleep for more than one day. I walked to the door, hoping that I'd find Jason on the other side. Of course it wasn't him. Instead, I was face to face with Ben who was sporting a bruised jaw and a busted lip.

I gasped and gently rubbed his jaw. "Oh my Lord! What happened to you?!"

Ben walked into the living room and took a seat on my sofa. "*Jason* happened to me."

I sat down beside him. "I'm so sorry, Ben."

"He was just upset." He kissed my forehead. "Where've you been? I've been trying to get in touch with you for a couple of days."

I patted the sofa. "I've been right here, asleep."

Ben pulled me into his arms. "I'm so sorry, sweetheart. Telling Jason about his father was just too much for you. I knew I should've been here when you told him."

I shook my head and softly kissed his lips. "It's alright. I knew he'd be upset." I backed out of Ben's arms and grasped both of his hands. "You'll never hurt me. You meant that, didn't you?"

He nodded. "Of course, I meant it."

I stood from the sofa and tugged on his hand. "Come with me."

He gave me a curious look as he stood and followed me into my bedroom.

He hesitated at the door and said, "Olivia, are you ready—"

I placed a finger to his lips and said, "Shh. Sit down."

Ben sat on the side of the bed and I leaned over and kissed first his bruised cheek, and then his swollen lips. "I love you, Ben," I whispered.

He cupped my face with his hands. "I love you, too. But I can't do this. It's not right. It feels like I'm taking advantage of you."

I stared into his eyes. I loved him so much. "Then will you just hold me? Hold me and never let me go."

He did just that. We lay in my bed and he held me close to his body, enveloping me in his warmth and his love. He held me until our heartbeats matched in rhythm. He didn't let me go.

~*~

That night, as I lay in Ben's arms, I thought about him, about Jason, and about David. The men in my life. I loved them all, I'd tried to protect them all, and I'd failed them all. I rubbed Ben's arm and then took his hand and kissed it.

"Can't sleep?" he asked.

"I think I've slept enough."

Ben kissed my forehead. "Hmm. I guess you're right."

I looked up at his face. "Ben, I need to tell you something."

He laced his fingers with mine and said, "Okay. What is it, sweetheart?"

"I need to tell you about the day David died—"

Ben interrupted me. "Don't do this to yourself, Olivia. You can't keep beating yourself up about that."

I sat up on the side of the bed. "Ben, please listen. *Please.*"

"Okay," he said softly.

"After I told David that I'd rather die than to become Ella again, he smiled and handed me the gun..."

*"Do it," he said. "I want to see you do it. Kill yourself."*

*I held the gun in my hand and stared at him.*

*"You can't, can you?"*

*I dropped my eyes to the floor.*

*He moved closer to me and placed his hand gently around my neck. I gasped, expecting him to choke me, but instead, he kissed my cheek and whispered in my ear, "So beautiful you still are, my Olivia. So beautiful...so beautiful. Do it, darling. Do it." He kissed my neck. "If you can't shoot yourself, then shoot me. Shoot me and free us both, darling."*

*I frowned and shook my head.*

*He laughed. "I knew you couldn't do it. You can't do anything!" He walked into the closet and pulled a video tape from one of the boxes. He sighed. "You're not Ella anymore. I need Ella. She makes me happy. You never could. I was never happy with Olivia. Only Ella," he said wistfully.*

*I followed him into the closet and looked at those boxes full of my* documented humiliation. I started to cry. *"I can't do it. I just can't. I can't be her. Please understand."*

He glared at me. *"I understand that you are weak! Look at you, sniveling like a pathetic little girl! I need a real woman. I NEED ELLA!"* He moved in close to me and placed his forehead against mine. *"Either you can do this willingly or I'll chain you to the damned bed and make you do it, but you WILL do it!"*

I can't really explain why I did what I did next. It was almost as if I was outside my body, watching myself as I lifted the gun and placed it at his temple. My finger trembled as I placed it on the trigger. *"David...please..."*

David smiled eerily as he put his hand over mine and softly said, *"What are you doing, darling?"*

*"I can't be Ella again. I cannot do it. I cannot...I cannot...I cannot..."* I said.

*"So, you're going to kill me? Go ahead, Olivia. Do it. Kill me or kill yourself, but do something and stop being so damned weak!"*

I stood there and stared at him. My heart raced and my own breathing was loud in my ears. I loved him so much. I loved him and I hated him. I needed him and I needed to be free of him. He was everything to me and he'd taken everything away from me.

His expression softened. *"If you loved me,"* he said softly. *"You'd kill me. You'd put me out of my misery." He placed his finger over mine and jiggled the trigger.*

*I wiped the tears from my face. "I do love you, David. And I always will," I whispered. When I pulled the trigger, a strange look came across his face. It was as if he was relieved...*

Ben frowned. "What...what are you saying, Olivia?"

"I'm telling you that David didn't commit suicide. I murdered him."

A deafening silence filled the room as Ben digested my words. After a few moments, he finally said, "Olivia, I..."

"I held him in my arms for two days before Jason found us. I held him and I cried for *two days*. Jason told the police that it was suicide. He knew David had been depressed. They never thought otherwise. No one thought I killed him, and I never confessed...until now."

"Olivia..."

I shook my head. "You don't have to say anything. I killed him, Ben. You can put it in the book or you can call the police. Either way, I'll understand. I just wanted you to know the truth."

Ben scooted over to my side of the bed and pulled me into his arms. "I love you, Olivia Moy, and nothing's going to change that. I don't care about the book. I care about you. David tormented and abused you and you ended it. I'm not calling the police. I'm not going to do anything but love you." Ben kissed me deeply and held me all night long.

The next morning, after both Ben and Jason left for work, I headed upstairs and slid an envelope underneath each of their doors. I then walked back down the stairs to my apartment, grabbed my bags, and took a taxi to the airport.

## *Twenty*

### "Think About You"

*I* glanced around the room, taking in the familiar faces. Faces of women whose pain I'd come to know well. Women who'd shared their pain with me and who'd readily accepted me and my own pain. I felt safe in that sterile-looking room. Safe enough to share my thoughts and fears. Safe enough to share my life and all that that meant. I adjusted in my seat and crossed my legs as one of the ladies, Katrina, spoke about her past. She was a new member of our group and her pain was fresh and raw. She reminded me of myself just a few months earlier.

"I want to heal so badly," Katrina said, her voice breaking. "I want to leave everything in the past."

Dr. Kimbrough, the group's facilitator, leaned forward and grasped Katrina's hand. "Healing is a process, Katrina. Any of the ladies here can tell you that. It's a process, not an overnight event."

Most of the ladies in the circle nodded. "Would anyone like to speak on this?" Dr. Kimbrough asked.

The room was silent for a moment. I decided to share what I'd learned. "Well, I think healing is an individual thing. We all heal differently, but the one common thing is acceptance. You have to accept who you are today and who you were in the past and you have to accept the events of the past in order to heal. For me, this took a lot of time and prayer. But I made it. Today I can honestly say that I'm healed and ready to move forward with my life."

I heard a chorus of "that's right" as several of the other women agreed with what I'd said. Katrina looked over at me and said, "I see what you're saying, but you don't understand what I've been through. I've tried to forget it and move on, but I can't."

I nodded. "You're right, I don't know exactly what you've been through, but I know that this is a group for women who've been abused, so I know that our stories must be similar. And as far as forgetting the past, you should never do that. Your past and my past made us who we are today. We'll never forget it. We can't, but we can accept it as what it is—the past. It's not the present or the future, so it has no business in the present nor the future. God readily forgives. We've got to do the same for ourselves."

The other ladies in the group agreed and Katrina gave me a thoughtful look as she too nodded in agreement. Our session went a little over the usual hour, but that didn't seem to bother anyone. I think all of us enjoyed our time of sharing. I know I did.

I gathered my purse and hugged a few of the ladies as I made my way to the door. Dr. Kimbrough stopped me before I could make my exit. "Olivia, can I speak to you for a moment?"

I smiled at her. "Of course."

She adjusted her glasses and returned my smile. "I just wanted to tell you how impressed I am with your progress. When you first came to me some months ago, you were so broken. Now I see such growth and strength. You are such an inspiration to the other participants. I think you'd make an excellent counselor. Have you thought about going back to school?"

I shook my head. "Oh, no. I have other plans. Big plans to help other women heal."

She nodded. "Well, I have no doubt that you'll be successful in all of your endeavors. So, are you still planning to move soon?"

I sighed. "I am. I love it here in Texas, but it's time for me to go back home. I've run from it long enough."

She rested her hand on my arm. "Well, we'll miss you. God bless you, Olivia."

"Thanks."

~*~

I sat in the living room full of boxes and sighed. I'd spent my life with David moving from place to place as he ran from a past full of pain that he'd never escape, but only perpetuate. I guess old habits really do die hard. I glanced out the window at the Dallas skyline. I'd moved to Dallas six months earlier, but the difference in me and David was that I wasn't running *from* anything. I was running *to* Dr. Melissa Kimbrough, one of the Christian counselors that were on the list Ben had given to me. I'd run to the beginning of a better life, peace of mind, and healing. Healing. What a peculiar word. A word with a different meaning for anyone who seeks it.

For some, healing comes in the form of suddenly being able to smile after an eternity of pain. For others, it might be finally getting a good night's sleep after a long period of insomnia. For me, healing came in the form of peace. Sweet, sweet peace. I remember the day so well. It was the first day that I could honestly say was devoid of any internal feelings of turmoil. I went through the entire day with no thoughts of the pain of the past, or of David's death, or of David at all. David Moy did not cross my mind even once that day. I felt so…so free. Free from the bondage that had held me captive for so long. Free from the prison of pain that had been my world for so many years. Free from the embarrassment and the shame. With that freedom, *true freedom*, I knew it was time for me to move forward with my life. Because, with David's absence from my mind, came Bennett Paul's presence.

Ben's face, his scent, and his smile inundated my thoughts. I felt his touch on my skin and his kiss on my lips. I missed him. *I loved him.* But I hadn't spoken to him since the day I left Chicago. I'd ignored his calls until he'd finally stopped calling. I'd once felt so unworthy of his love, but now I craved it. *I loved Bennett Paul.*

I was jerked out of my thoughts as my cell phone began to buzz and dance across the top of one of the boxes. I hoped it was Jason or Ben. I'd tried to call Jason several times to no avail. I'd been too ashamed to call Ben. I checked the screen and gasped. It was Jason. I eagerly pressed the button to accept the call and said, "Hello? Jason?"

"M...Mother?" His voice was so soft I barely heard him.

I closed my eyes as they filled with tears. "Yes? Jason, how've you been?"

"I'm okay. I'm sorry, Mother. I'm so, so sorry." His voice wavered and my tears fell more furiously.

"It's alright, son. I understand."

"No. No it's not. I was so angry at you. I believed the things Father had told me about you. He...he was my hero."

"I know, dear. I never wanted to ruin your image of him."

"Mother, I read Ben's book...all of it."

I was silent. I honestly didn't know what to say.

"It just made me angrier. I couldn't believe it. I was so upset, I flew to Arkansas. I wanted to prove that you'd made it all up. I went to the house and…and…"

"Jason—"

"I saw the boxes. The tapes. So many of them…" I could hear him as he began to sob. "I watched one of them."

I held my hand to my mouth. "Oh, Jason, no. I never wanted you to see me like that. *No…*"

"I couldn't watch it all. Mother, oh God! I'm so sorry. I'm so sorry…" He was sobbing loudly into the phone.

"Jason…Jason listen. Listen to me. Your father was very ill. If you read the entire book then you know that he was a victim of abuse himself. It was all he knew. He needed help. If I'd known that, things would've been different."

"Mother, did he really try to kill me when I was a baby."

I closed my eyes. "I never wanted you to know that. I really didn't. I should never have told Ben. Now the world will know."

"No, they won't. He's not publishing it."

I frowned. "What?"

"He gave me all of the copies of his manuscript and his flash drive. He said he couldn't do it. That it was your private business."

"He did?"

"Yes, and he said to tell you that your secrets are safe with him. All of them."

It was my turn to sob into the phone.

"Mother, he was so hurt and worried after you left. Even though I was angry at him, he begged me to tell him where you were. I told him I didn't know. I'm sorry I didn't answer your calls before. I just needed to get my head together."

I wiped my eyes. "I understand. Um, Jason, is Ben home right now?"

"No, he moved a couple of months ago. He just quit his job, signed the building over to me, and left."

"Where'd he go?"

"California, to be near his son. I was wrong about him, you know. He really loves you. I could say it a million times and it still wouldn't make a difference, but I really am sorry, Mother. I really, truly am."

I sighed. "It's okay, love. We all live and learn."

"Mother, how are you doing now?"

We talked for hours, catching each other up on the past months of our lives. When I hung up, I cried tears of joy and pain. I was so happy to have reconciled with my son. I'd missed him and I loved him so much. But, there was still Ben. With him missing from my life, a piece of me was missing. I closed my eyes and prayed that we'd find our way back to one another. I prayed that one day he'd know just how much I loved him.

*Twenty-One*

## "Forever, For Always, For Love"

"*I'd* like to introduce our benefactor for tonight. The president of our organization's board of directors, Ms. Olivia Moy."

I thanked the mistress of ceremonies and then took her place behind the podium. "Thank you all for sharing this special night with me and my son. We established the David Moy Foundation in order to assist those who have endured abuse of any kind to find healing and to live better lives. My late husband, whom the foundation was named after, was a victim of abuse as a child. So this cause is very near and dear to the hearts of the Moy family."

I paused and smiled at David's father who sat right next to Jason. "Our plan is to establish counseling centers in cities throughout the country, starting here in Memphis, David's hometown. As you know, our motto is: Helping the Hurt to Heal. Thank you all so much for partnering with us and celebrating with us. Please enjoy the rest of your evening."

I smiled as I left the platform amidst applause from the audience.

I made my way back to my table and was greeted with a kiss from Jason. I hugged him and his new fiancé, Sandra, and took my seat across from them. I placed my napkin in my lap and was about to dig into my Chicken Parmesan, when I felt someone settle into the seat next to mine. The familiar scent of Dial soap and Jergen's lotion filled my nose and at the same time, tears filled my eyes.

I looked up at him and shook my head. Was I seeing things? And if I was, could this vision please go on forever? "Oh my God," I whispered.

A smile spread across his face. "No, just me."

I nodded and tried not to cry. I tried really hard, made a valiant effort, gave it all I had, but I still cried.

Ben reached over and wiped my face with his napkin. "No tears tonight. This is a celebration, right?"

I nodded. "Ben, I am so sorry for leaving like that and losing touch."

He placed a finger to my lips to silence me. "In the letter you left me, you said you needed to help yourself, to find some healing. Did you find it?"

I looked at his beautiful face. "I did. I really did."

He grasped my hand in his then leaned forward and kissed me

softly. "I love you, Olivia."

"You still love me?"

He gently caressed my cheek. "I'll *always* love you."

"I love you too, Ben. There hasn't been a day you haven't crossed my mind. I love you so much."

He smiled as he brought my hand to his lips and kissed it. "I love you and you love me, so what are we going to do about this?"

I smiled and softly kissed his lips. "We are going to spend the rest of our lives loving each other. I don't want to spend another second of my life without you in it."

He hugged me tightly. "Neither do I."

## Ode to Olivia

Truly a beauty never beheld

Such sweet innocence she evokes

Such serenity surrounds her being

Loveliness unmatched, a unique magnificence

Her heart consumes me with every beat

She is synonymous with splendor

The very essence of bliss

Warm brown skin, I've found, is my addiction.

Lips so full, so anxious for mine

I close my eyes, her breath beckons my surrender

It is she, not me, who matters

I feel her touch from afar

Knowing every line and ridge of her fingerprint

Committing to memory every inch of her beauty

Her soft murmurs and moans are a symphony to my ears

She is all

She is everything

It is Olivia and Olivia alone that I need

My greatest desire is her nearness

Olivia is my divine pleasure


-David A. Moy

For more information on Domestic Violence, go to:

**http://www.domesticviolence.org/**

For information about the author, go to:

**http://adriennethompsonwrites.webs.com**

Adrienne would love to hear from you! Feel free to email her at:

**tapestrywriter@gmail.com**

Or connect with her on Facebook:

**https://www.facebook.com/pages/Author-Adrienne-Thompson/300208429995218**

Or Twitter:

**@A_H_Thompson**

Excerpt from:

*Little Sister* (Cleo's Story)

A Companion Novel to Been So Long

(Coming Soon)

I crouched over the toilet in the grimy gas station restroom, trying to keep my balance as I relieved myself. I eyed the graffiti-riddled stall walls and door, reading the various markings. *Wherever you go, there you are....Jill was here...Jesus is love...suck my*—well, you get the gist of it. After I finished, I stepped out of the stall to the sink, where I washed my hands and dried them on my jeans. No paper towels, no hand drier. I pushed the door open and walked back out into the station. The aroma of old fried chicken and old chicken grease filled my nose. I eyed the food in the warmer and although the chicken looked dry—almost petrified, I wished for a piece.

I reached in my pocket and pulled out the twenty dollars I'd taken from my mother's purse. I'd been walking the highway for six hours. All I'd had for breakfast was a pop tart and some orange juice. I'd skipped lunch altogether, so that dry chicken seemed more like a huge slice of greasy pepperoni pizza to me..

I ordered a two-piece meal and slid onto one of the two benches situated in what amounted to the convenience store's restaurant. I was so hungry and so engrossed with filling my stomach, that I didn't even notice that the man sitting across from me was staring at me. All I cared about was the leg and thigh that I had drenched with hot sauce. I took a big bite and nearly swallowed the meat without chewing it. I took a gulp of orange soda before finishing the chicken leg in two more bites.

I was entranced with eating the old chicken, stale roll, and rock-hard okra—transfixed with the satisfying fullness that I felt. I sat there and licked my fingertips before polishing off my soda. I stood from the bench and rubbed my hands on the thighs of my jeans. As I headed out of the gas station, my legs felt as heavy as my eyelids. My full belly had zonked my energy, and as I continued my hours-long trek down the highway towards nowhere in particular, I moved much slower than I had at the beginning of my journey.

At twilight, I started to think about finding somewhere to sleep for the first time that day. Being a twelve year-old, I had not planned things out too well, and now, as I walked along the shoulder of Highway 67, the darkening Arkansas sky began to frighten me. I glanced towards the dense trees that lined the highway and my imagination began to see lit eyes in the darkness. What if there was a bear or a werewolf in there? What if there was an ax murderer hiding out in the woods?

I pulled my thin windbreaker around my body and rubbed my hands up and down my arms as the fall evening air began to chill me. I had to figure out some place to sleep. I shoved my hand into the hip pocket of my jeans and felt the fifteen dollars that I had left. That, along with a backpack full of Cheetos, Pop Tarts, and oranges, was all I had with me. Well, that and the three outfits I had packed.

I was so deep in thought, that I didn't hear the truck when it pulled to a stop on the shoulder. By now I was used to the noise of the highway, the sound of cars whizzing by or the loud horns of the big rigs, so a truck braking behind me didn't concern me. I continued to walk and ponder my situation when I heard a voice behind me.

"Hey, little sister! Where you headed?!"

I frowned but I didn't turn around. He couldn't have been speaking to me.

"Hey, little girl!"

I stopped in my tracks and turned around. I didn't answer him because I still wasn't sure he was talking to me. The voice came from the man I'd seen at the gas station. The one who was sitting across from me. He was tall with skin the color of a Snicker's bar. He smiled and repeated himself. "Where you going?"

I shrugged.

"You don't know?"

I shrugged again. I remembered my grandmother telling me not to ever talk to strangers. That was before she moved away, but I still remembered it. I remembered everything she ever told me. This man was a stranger, so I wasn't about to talk to him.

"Can't talk?" he asked.

Another shrug from me.

"Wanna ride?"